Meer
a novel

Humra Quraishi

RUPA

Published by
Rupa Publications India Pvt. Ltd 2015
7/16, Ansari Road, Daryaganj
New Delhi 110002

Sales Centres:

Allahabad Bengaluru Chennai
Hyderabad Jaipur Kathmandu
Kolkata Mumbai

Copyright © Humra Quraishi 2015

This is a work of fiction. Names, characters, places and incidents are
either the product of the author's imagination or are used fictitiously and
any resemblance to any actual person, living or dead,
events or locales is entirely coincidental.

All rights reserved.
No part of this publication may be reproduced, transmitted,
or stored in a retrieval system, in any form or by any means,
electronic, mechanical, photocopying, recording or otherwise,
without the prior permission of the publisher.

ISBN: 978-81-291-2400-5

First impression 2015

10 9 8 7 6 5 4 3 2 1

The moral right of the author has been asserted.

Printed by HT Media Ltd, Noida

This book is sold subject to the condition that it shall not,
by way of trade or otherwise, be lent, resold, hired out, or otherwise circulated,
without the publisher's prior consent, in any form of binding or
cover other than that in which it is published.

Meer

Humra Quraishi is a Delhi-based writer-columnist-journalist. Her books include *Kashmir: The Untold Story*; a volume of her collective writings, *Views: Yours and Mine*; and a short-story collection, *More Bad Time Tales*. She has co-authored *The Good, The Bad and The Ridiculous: Profiles, Absolute Khushwant* and a series of writings with the late Khushwant Singh. She has also contributed to the anthologies, *Chasing the Good Life: On Being Single* and *Of Mothers and Others*.

*For all those surviving in the
conflict zones of this subcontinent.*

Prelude

I begin to crawl in the lock-up. Then sit back restless, then crawl once again. Repeatedly. In this hellhole, I am on all fours, my breasts dangling and looking pathetic. Drooping and disdainful. Outcast, downcast. But for what? I'm rebuking them just like the men who'd pushed and pulled, grasped and clasped my breasts.

Suddenly, they're alive again! Responding to those distant cries which seem to be coming from another plane miles away…those cries hitting where they hurt the most. My fragile breasts. I squat, as though set to deliver, to let go of the flesh tucked inside me. And then no longer can I sit still. I writhe on the bare floor, like I had done that night, months ago. The only difference was that it was a wooden floor. And that I wasn't alone when I lay sapped of all energy in that bloody mess. As the secretions rolled down my thighs, provoking my uterus and ovaries to join in that rebellious outburst, I lay helplessly on the floor of the dunga parked along the Jhelum. Writhing—till I could no longer hear the cries of my newborn.

I turn abruptly as the images gain momentum, naïvely expecting that the exercise will be enough to yoke their flow. That distinct image of a child emerging from my inner folds, crying... It's too much to bear. I put my bony fingers to my ears, imploring those cries to go away.

Even in this jailed state, I don't let go of the charges thrown at me—those two crumpled chits found on me, together with the two dead forms—a newborn, and the other just a few months old.

I feel the interrogators' cold eyes on my face. 'You say you're Husna Hakeem—who's this other person whose name is on the chit? Are you a Hakeem woman or are you Deepti Kaul? Have you converted or are you reconverting? Who gave you these two chits...these two names?' The questions are unrelenting and their voices menacing.

They don't listen when I speak. They don't want to. Even as I continue to tell them that I was handed those chits to counter hurdles at some stage of the turbulence.

'What turbulence? And the two dead bodies? You killed them, didn't you?'

'Killed by those shooting and killing and ...'

'These dead harami pillas are yours?'

'No. They pulled out my baby from my womb in that dunga.'

'Whose are these then?'

'One is to be buried and that other one was thrown at my chest. Meer would have called them destiny's children.'

'Who is Meer? Give us his full name, address, his occupation.'

'Meer did nothing!'

'House number, street number?' they yell.

'No house. He lives in a dunga along the embankment. My child was born there, but I couldn't even hold my own child.'

'You and that man producing children! You people haven't been sterilized?'

'Today even strays are not sterilized!' I hiss back.

'So what're you up to? Planning something big? Why're you visiting this sensitive place again and again?'

'I've come only twice—in 1992, and now. I landed only last evening to search for him and for my child!'

'Killed or kidnapped?'

'Pulled away from me!' I wail.

'These two chits with two names—were they handed to you at the airport?'

'Meer gave me these chits long before I was kicked out of here…said that these were for my safety. I have been keeping them safe all these months.'

'Come on, give us more details before you are kicked again.' They start kicking me frantically and all I can mumble are the few facts I know. I keep trying to move away amidst those screams and threats…the interrogators keep gaping at me and my form moving about on all fours. Taking a break before resuming the job of breaking my back and much more.

※

Restlessness overtakes me as I loosen the string holding up my shalwar and roll it down to my thighs. I pull up my kurta, almost throttling my neck, baring my protruding stomach and crestfallen breasts to the mosquitoes, which swarm around me like the lecherous old men with their leftover reserves of desire. Patting my stomach, I feel the fibrous growth in me. It has been lying nestled there for years and has now become a part of my anatomy. No caressing of the breasts lying flat; long neglected, sullen, sad and saddled with no particular emotions nor want, none of those yearnings for foreplay and wrap-ups. No one around to clasp, hug or fuck. After all, lovers are not like sacks of potatoes you'd pick up from a bustling mandi.

Inhibitions drilled early in life are difficult to let go. Tightening the string of my tattered and stained shalwar, deadening my urges, I crawl around, wailing and crying.

No, no special treatment for me, even as I cry aloud. I pull the tatters around me closer. Restless, as though the waters of the Jhelum had flooded the embankment and seeped right into the backyard of my erstwhile home—that dunga, unmoving, as though stranded atop those waters.

I sit up with a sudden start when those fleeting images can no longer be contained—somewhat demolished and abolished with the superimposed images of that search on that crackdown night. I can see the fragments of broken glass and newspaper shreds flung around me as I'd lain in the corner. In the frame, I see the blurred faces of those men—standing hunched in a row all along the street overlooking the embankment. It was as though this exercise had stripped them of all the manly exercises they'd earlier indulged in. Hadn't Meer repeatedly muttered a volley of disgust? That look of humiliation in his eyes...that look of utter helplessness. Hunched he'd stood, even when the dunga was encircled that night. The images lurk around me. Those men barging in, searching and destroying. The more frantic their search became, the wilder my screams grew. But it didn't make even a dent on their hardened psyches. Pulling and pushing, they gaped as I thrust out the life from my pelvis.

My hands quiver. I fling them around, weeping bitterly. When was the last time I'd flung them about? It was that night—in the midst of that crackdown, writhing in pain as the mass of flesh pushed against me to emerge from my form. My child, my newborn!

I look down at my breasts. They lie drooping, as though defeated in purpose and want. My uterus feels like it is churning in an uncontrolled fashion, indulging in a mourning session, as if to join in the mass revolt.

My agonized cries gain momentum. But suddenly they are drowned by the shrill shrieks from the adjoining cell. They are an assortment of strange pleas, 'Throw me back...back to Ali Zai...away from here... back to my Ali Zai mohalla... I'm no terrorist, only half-Afghan! No terrorist!'

The voice sounds familiar. I have heard it before. Yes, I am sure I have. But whose voice is it? Where had I heard it? Where could I have heard it? And who could be yearning to go to Ali Zai mohalla? Isn't that the mohalla tucked away in Shahjahanpur? That Avadhi township where my mother's clan survived amidst all possible hurdles? Where they had settled down after travelling from Afghanistan?

I crawl towards the cell, craning my neck to catch a glimpse of that imprisoned woman, but it is impossible to see her. I can just hear those shrieks getting shriller, those desperate pleas begging to be transported back to Ali Zai.

I wait to hear that cry once again. It starts as a slow wail building into a full-throated volley, like raw apples falling on the skull. 'I can't breathe...throw me back...take me back ...I am only half an Afghan. Not a terrorist!'

Could she be ShahNoor khala? But how? How could she be here in this adjoining cell in the Valley? The more I listen to the voice, the more I'm certain that it is ShahNoor khala's voice...her frenzied cries, hysterical outbursts to be transported back. Why did I have to hear her voice now? Why, after all these years? Why couldn't I ever let go of the image of her face? Of her?

Even after three decades ShahNoor khala's face emerges in periodical flashes in front of me. Those large eyes with that strange stillness. Her motionless presence tore apart the stillness. She'd lie still, day after day, in that hot summer stretch, with nothing left to tear her apart. It was through her that I'd witnessed that fierce intensity early in my childhood. I was too young to comprehend the complexities, but was old enough to grasp the undercurrent of those sabotaged yearnings, to witness and sense those frustrations fuming within.

As the sluggish passenger train carrying us from Bareilly to Shahjahanpur came to a halt, the hold on our hands by the elders lessened to grip the holdalls, to descend on the railway platform of that nondescript town in Avadh. It signalled the beginning of our annual summer vacation in my mother's ancestral haveli, surrounded by vast acres of agricultural land and a wider ring of shanties around it.

This time around, it wasn't the usual summer. Sometime during it, ShahNoor khala had rebelled. She lay hapless on the terrace, her rebelliousness seething under the summer sun. Scorched. Just as she was scorned by the clan—the clan that boasted its Afghan blood.

All these years those images of her supine form on that bare terrace, under the raging sun, remain unmoving in my mind. Just as unmoving as those lurking doubts, those strange twists and turns, reactions and theories. How did we just sit—like an impotent bunch? How did we not react or help move her away from the ruthless sun unleashing its wrath on her form till it ebbed each evening at dusk?

We returned the next summer. She was nowhere to be seen. The whispers by the servants suggested that she'd walked away, out of the haveli's darwaza, towards another township. Their mutters relayed that she'd bothered little about family ties and the stifling regrets that go along with it…she had eloped with a Kashmiri and with that disappeared like the Sufis of yesteryears…vanishing, never ever to reappear. But for some strange unfathomable reason, the memories hovering around her have held sway over me all these years. It is as though she lies alive somewhere deep, well-buried, in my psyche.

There are memories, too, of those two others of my clan who lie buried in that parched earth. My younger brother Fareed and my aged father Hussain Hakeem, lying in the folds of the ever-consuming earth, with its maddening urge to consume more dead forms than it could hold.

Hurriedly buried in a graveyard in Bareilly, which now has so many dead that it had become impossible for me to trace the graves that I was looking for. 'Not one qabristan in this city that is cemented…only kutcha graves that merge…' the graveyard keepers said eerily, as though to forewarn me.

Merging with all those other graves. Those of people hacked by those rioters. What Alzheimer's couldn't do, those rioters did. Wrecking my father's chiselled face and those remaining memory cells. The rest of those cells had already shrunk with an alarming pace, leaving just enough patches floating about the brain along a polka-dotted strain. He'd tried to battle those faint traces of memories that emerged every now and then, as though to nudge the deep reservoirs of memory that all's not over yet—till the time the rioters closed in on him, sliding under the ledge, swiftly shifting to the outer hedge. The wild rioters unleashed their fury on those mango trees that surrounded the kothi and far beyond. Forms fell apart like ripened fruit, pregnant and full, succumbing to those onslaughts from the courtyard to the thereafter.

Restless and agitated, as though being laid, or rather waylaid, in this hellhole, amidst layers of security—a bandobast seemingly fractured by the constant shifts and somersaults of political whims. Secure forms quite simply bought over; doubling with rescued urchins or else singularly sprawled to be masturbating as never before, with crooked fingers overdoing the release along that dubiously infected parched terrain.

I look around at those others queuing up to be interrogated, barely visible through the slit-like window. As the names and addresses of those rounded up ricochet from the bare walls, the postures worsen. Bewildered and baffled like subdued cattle; technically innocent, yet to be dumped as undertrials or to be forcibly put on trial or to be hung by the noose, using those special acts and amendments. All on flimsy made-up allegations.

Several forms dragged by their hair or whatever else grew on their skulls, unsettling those remains on mine… I couldn't cry out even when I saw the several detained becoming uncontrollable—biting at their own skin and flesh rather than waiting for the trained interrogators to do so.

The mind has its own peculiar way of settling, or rather unsettling, the past with the present. It spreads through the blurred images of the stubby fingers of the security force, pressing down on my form inside that dunga where I'd lain writhing in the last stage of labour. With the rest of the fingers lingering on my chest, their forefingers pointed at the figures moving around not too far, around the bend of the embankment. They'd touched me and patted my breasts, hips, inner thighs, moved under there…pulling out that brassiere stitched and restitched at the sides, tugging that not-so-white bloodstained shalwar. And after scrutinizing the semi-torn faded panty, with holes riddled mercilessly in those scanty interiors, they were probably finally exhausted by the very business of checking and counter-checking, and moved away.

As those images of my privates getting very publicly displayed can't be contained, I vomit, flowing and overflowing like a sewage disaster. I can't turn as my ribs seem to be breaking… I can't shriek out, for that would have given them reasonable ground for shifting me from here to there. Or even shifting themselves into my inner folds.

The images choke me. Going backwards again to that

crackdown night when those men stormed in, throwing about cracked cups and much more. I'd begun to toss from one end of the wooden floor to the other. I pulled at my long tresses, clawed at my own flesh and shrieked as though I was a goat whose slim throat was being slit steadily, with that razor-sharp knife finding its way through the skin and veins. As the crackdown gained momentum, my shrieks became wilder. And just when I had begun to bang my hands on the wooden floor, my inner voice came through, as though trying to reach out.

Directed at me.

Directly at me. Cajoling me to throw up my legs. To just somehow do away with the obstructions in the pelvic contours.

Unable to contain any further onslaught of those memories tucked away, I sit back in this lock-up, but those pent-up images waft in front of me—somehow unmoving from the Kashmir Valley, where I had first landed months ago and now again, a second time, an evening ago.

Both times I travelled to the Valley for a specific reason, triggered by the demolition of the Babri Masjid.

Who can say that the Babri Masjid demolition was just the demolition of a mere structure?

That turbulent aftermath demolished fragile forms and ruined many a human life. And changed the entire course of mine.

Chapter 1

Crawling in this cell, crawling through those thoughts furthering, stretching out much further, towards my hometown Bareilly. Could I be once again thrown back to my hometown Bareilly? Would it be renamed Braeli or Breilly or even Billy-Town by those political monsters hell-bent on bringing changes to the world order? It was that one lone visit by someone from the Clinton clan to inaugurate that AIDS Adda that got them to think along that Billy-Town format.

Would my hometown Bareilly remain in Uttar Pradesh or be shifted to the freshly formulated state of Western Avadh? Or will it be clubbed with those towns stacked along the Union Territory? What would be left of our ancestral place? Would I be able to manage anything? Who could I search for? I had gone about searching for those graves in those graveyards but couldn't locate any containing my father's or my brother's dead forms. For that matter, could I ever manage to reach there on my own? I was thrown into that police van by those cops, without any deadly encounters taking place on the way.

The images washed over me—the scarecrows along our orchard stretch guarding those mango trees laden with langras, dusehris, fajris, chausas, totaparees, safaidas and husnaras. More images. Of those stretched-out branches overladen with mangoes. My brother and I climbing the branches. Plucking mangoes effortlessly. Swaying on the branches in those hot summer months as the devastating loo—hot May winds—went about hitting our faces, slapping our cheeks, flirting unashamedly with that mul duppatta flung rather too regularly across my chest. No, the breasts were not overpowering enough to beckon them.

Intrusions creep into my being at an alarming pace. Trying to figure out the sequence. Hitting me forcefully with more from the past. Chalk marks and nameplates, demolitions and their aftermath. That December evening of 1992, when the censored shots of the Babri Masjid demolition started pervading the small screen.

Earlier—that is, prior to 1992—any happenings in and about, big or small, would inevitably get linked to that partitioning year of 1947. Though for a great majority that period was part of history textbooks, it was not so in my home. The Partition held sway and continued with its hold. Whilst cutting through mangoes, my father would inevitably murmur about his two siblings, Iftikhar and

Zulfikhar, who had crossed those borders. Would they be able to buy these aams of varying varieties? Saying that, he would walk towards the mango trees. He often looked lost and forlorn then, as though he'd actually gone about looking for those long gone. In the last few years he'd used those orchards for those walkaway sessions…reduced to a restless someone seeking refuge among those trees. From home to those orchards stretching on the outskirts of the kothi built on the outskirts of the town. Even when struck with Alzheimer's, he could make out the difference between those varieties—langras, dusehris, fajris, chausas, totaparees, safaidas and husnaras. He could tell one from the other. He could make out the khaandaanis from the ordinary, compare tight-bodied dusehri mangoes from those pulp-soaked chausaas, just as he'd compared family backgrounds of those lurking around my family. Right till the end, he kept brushing aside any marriage proposal for me, saying that 'the best have crossed over to the new country—what kind of liaisons can be formed with the leftover third-class khurchans, those kameens lingering around?' He looked down on any intermingling with them. My father would take pains to narrate, rather too often, rather too endlessly, how his cousin Laddan mian married off his daughter Amreen to that bureaucrat babu without finding out about the clan. His words dripped with bitterness, 'How he treats her! How he controls those rupees! Don't know whether she'd die of tuberculosis or malnutrition…kameena babu…no idea which gullee he's from…it will affect generations to come…'

The winter of 1992 took over all the Partition pains of 1947. The saffron brigade invaded our home, together with those khaki-clad knickerwallahs. They had gone about unleashing terror. I recall that bay window falling, succumbing to the fury of those rioters. The outer doors and windows of our home were pounded and broken into. The little bakery we had set up at one end of the sprawling compound was set on fire, burning the bread along with the bakers.

My plaits were pulled back much before my brother's arms were broken. Just about when those three Kashmiri Muslim boys had pulled down the chiks inside the bakery, naïvely trying to cover their identity. Shrieking as they were killed…as my Alzheimer's-stricken father's fading memory cells burst hollow into shreds. Trishuls poked about here and there, where those cells lay shrinking. His smashed skull lay near the bakery furnace. Amidst much noise, quiet lay those cries and shrieks of those connected and the not so. Scaring away the scarecrows, and pulling down trees, the charged goons had barged into the courtyard of our home, converting the alive into the long list of the dead. Amidst horrifying slogans, 'Out Kashmiri terrorists, out with these Musalmaans! Out of this very best bakery!'

Not even one fleeting glance of a fleeing form did I see as I stumbled towards the connecting lanes that led to the inner folds of the old city. All the doors and windows were shut and clamped at the ghanta-ghar roundabout. Rows of dwellings stood erect, but just about.

I had banged these hands on the heavy iron darwaza of Aleem-Taleem madrasa, which was still standing, but to no avail. I ran further down the municipality-run park, towards the dak khana, and banged these hands on yet another darwaza of yet another madrasa, calling out to Maulvi Imam Baksh Ansari who'd come every alternate day to teach Urdu to my brother Fareed, as schools in Uttar Pradesh had made quite sure to wipe it clean off the charter of their syllabi. No, none of those mother tongue frills for those Musalmaan bachchas.

From the slit-like window the maulvi sahib had squeaked. By then, he seemed well-equipped with a certain amount of grit to move away from that window to the door. To squeak more along with two others. Beard ends and hands moved about in nervous quivers, 'The police are around. You're Fareed's apa? Why are you here? The sipahis are around. They just shooed off that Kashmiri shawl-wallah. He'd come running here for refuge…but we couldn't keep him. Not safe…no longer safe. He left his stack of shawls here…take some.'

With that, those quivers gained momentum in between flinging out those shawls one by one.

Some fell on my feet.

Several near them.

Others first hit my face before falling to a heap on the muddy lane.

Shooing me off! Was I a bitch in heat, desperate to release hormonal turbulence there and then? There was nothing to go back to. Except to get raped or hacked to death. If only I could stay on in this madrasa…

But they were unyielding. Nervous and rattling. 'A woman here! Sipahis here five times a day. Not for namaaz!' Their voices ebbed, 'Run, run away, never be seen in this gullee…take these shawls, sell them along the way. You look like a Kashmiri, run from here…save yourself!' The voices urged me to go away.

Maulvi sahib dug deep into one end of his faded kurta and threw out a couple of one hundred rupee notes. Were they the same crumpled notes my father had handed him for last month's tuition charges?

'Where do I go?'

'Go to hell…out of here!'

'To my mother's town Shahjahanpur or…'

'No, no… Dangaas, maardhaar spreading.'

'Hide me…someplace here please,' I begged.

'Run to Kanyakumari or Kashmir…you look like a Kashmiri.'

'That shawl-wallah…where? His sons were killed along with my father and…'

'Heard all that! Don't repeat those details, otherwise murder charges will be on my head! That shawl-wallah has been stuffing rupees into Daroga sahib's pockets. Saw with my own eyes. These eyes have seen too much.'

'Where's he?'

'Must be running towards Kashmir saving his skull. What's left here?'

'He's running all the way to Kashmir?'

'You run too—stuff yourself into some bus before they drag you somewhere.'

'But these rupees and…'

'Here, take another hundred and get out. Sell these shawls on the way. Out of this hell!'

Counting and recounting the rupees clutched in my hand, I walked the one-kilometre stretch to queue at the bus ticket counter. Boarding a big-bodied bus that took long and shortcuts through the plains of North India to finally halt on the outskirts of the city of Jammu.

It was well past midnight but there was no sign of the start-off from Jammu. There was a problem with the brakes of the bus, they said. Around dawn the bus started moving. We were on our way to Srinagar.

Before the man sitting in the next seat could stop throwing up, the one next to him had begun poking his forefinger into his beak-shaped nose. The sight was nauseating. I distracted myself by peering out of the window, which brought me little relief as by then the bus lurched to a stop off the highway near a deep ditch.

The brakes had failed. This time permanently. The driver and conductor were busy trying to get another bus from an adjoining depot, announcing in between that it could be a while for the bus to arrive so passengers were free to walk around and stretch their legs.

After a while, the passengers became impatient and when they got no answers from the driver, they were fuming. Soon another bus arrived. It was a minibus with half the number of the required seats and a quarter of that willpower to carry us through the journey.

I sat atop a rusted tin trunk, one hand firmly placed on my chest and the other clutching one of the iron bars jutting out from one end of the adjoining seat...till the bar came into my hand, throwing me onto the lap of an ageing man sitting not too far on a makeshift bundle. A bundle of nerves, if nothing else! He screamed...and continued to do so, blaming me for fracturing his ribs! Of course, there were no doctors aboard the bus to harness these disasters. Only a couple of quacks quaking...compounding the noise pollution. I quickly pulled off my dupatta from my drooping breasts to tie it around the chest of this man who was doubling up in pain! There was no way that this minibus would halt for these mini emergencies.

But the minibus did halt. A kilometre or so before the outer city limits of Srinagar. It had to. The road had caved in! There were several other vehicles stranded there. Some passengers were brave enough to venture ahead on foot while others like me stuffed themselves into a matador parked on the other side.

As the matador finally braked close to the gates of the Tourist Reception Centre, passengers walked out, weary and hunched. I drew strange looks from the locals. Perhaps

I looked an outsider, a stranger in search...of that shawl-seller whose sons had been brutally killed. No, I couldn't cart the dead forms of his teenage sons; I could barely carry myself, escaping from the ruins of my ancestral place, my home, from the clutches of the goons holding sway.

※

I roamed the streets of Srinagar, trying to locate that shawl-seller. I had no clue about his whereabouts. Simply called Kashmiri shawl-wallah, I had no idea what his name, surname or even address was. He'd always breezed in and out of our home with a stack of shawls and an offbeat story to offload. He'd sit under that cluster of trees and show us one shawl after another, explaining the patterns around each. Halting only to gulp down chai, flowing from the kitchen chullah built close to the courtyard's outer end, not too far from the makeshift bakery shed. Our cook Idris would be pottering around, his hands moving from the sil batta to shredding onions for the do-pyaza to throwing tea leaves into that twisted boiler. He hated intrusions, and did not take lightly to even any mundane suggestions, big or small. Just once, this shawl-seller had happened to bring along a kahwa packet, and got permission to make the special brew—Kashmiri chai—for us, but Idris had fumed so ferociously that the seller had had little option but to get back to the weaves and patterns of his shawls.

He would fix his base at Bareilly and travel by bus to

the smaller towns—Shahjahanpur, Badaun, Haldwani, Hardoi, Sitapur, Sandila, Shahbad, Lakhimpur Kheri. Or to those other outlying qasbas and mufassils. A bicycle was out of the question—what with the official woven theories of bombs being planted on them by bombing agencies. Not that travelling by bus in North India was very easy for a Kashmiri, but there was no option—he would bribe his way through by gifting a shawl or two here and there. That was a small price to pay for being allowed to move around freely and not be taken for a terrorist or at least be labelled one to be slaughtered in a fake encounter. He'd travelled on Uttar Pradesh's not-so-sarkari fleet of rickety four-wheelers too, to peddle his shawls.

In between weaves and patterns, he'd weave stories around each shawl his hands held out, gesturing abundantly to explain those intricate details. Tales that were laced and interlaced with the realities of the day. We'd wait for the shawl-selling season that started around November and went on till February-end. He'd disappear into the Valley soon after, as though curling back into some sort of self-imposed hibernation. He'd hinted about a rundown café on the embankment that he ran all through the summer, but come autumn he'd be back. Right there. With those shawls.

And that winter, when he'd come to our home, with him was not just his usual stack of shawls but three young boys—his teenage sons, Kareem, Raheem and Faheem. He asked if they could stay with us for a week or two till he'd travelled around those outlying locales. He told us that hostels run by Muslims didn't want Kashmiri Muslim children because of the enthusiastic police and intelligence agencies hounding and waiting to pin terrorist tags on them. He hinted that he couldn't risk leaving them anywhere because the police would more than just probe his young sons. But why did he drag them from the Valley to be thrown in here? He had openly spoken of the rising number of boys disappearing in the Valley and thrown into the 'missing' slots.

After a short while of apparent tension, my father nodded, giving in to his earnest pleas. They—the three boys—looked gloomy, sitting on the lawn, not really venturing too far…only till the bakery, in fact, even helping to bake the bread, buns and biscuits we supplied to the neighbourhood. Quiet and subdued, they quickly brushed off any queries with some smart-ass responses—things that they seemed to have been trained to say, presumably by their father. They had a faraway look in their eyes. Perhaps a forewarning of a kind.

※

And whilst on that lookout for that shawl-seller on the roads of Srinagar, I saw that same deadened faraway look in many pairs of eyes. In that shawl-weavers' mohalla, in the congested downtown area and in the lanes and by-lanes. I walked for hours and my feet were swollen to such an extent that my sandals had started hurting me. I hired an autorickshaw in exchange for one of the shawls. The driver tried to take me to the shawl weavers that could fit the descriptions I wove from the back seat. Driving from one filth-laden lane to the next, from one locality to the next, from one discarded loom to the next...till the young driver braked near a man who was sitting absolutely still. He didn't even turn to look. No, not even when the driver spoke with him in Kashmiri. He just mumbled and pointed towards another man sitting not too far away. Even that man had no enthusiasm to direct any further. Just pointed to another of those hunched weavers, who too didn't have anything to say. Where all that auto-driver took me! It was impossible to recollect those details. The metre showed over a 100 kilometres by the time we halted somewhere on the outskirts of the municipal limits of the city. It had rained and the kutcha road was broken in some parts. Even in that barrenness, I could see strangely twisted sprouts making their way out. The convoys kept passing us by as the auto kept stopping. We couldn't overtake them otherwise we'd be ripped apart.

More than the wilderness, it was his unwillingness to drive me back to the city that made me go about in circles. Finally, he drove back towards the city centre, towards the Zero Bridge.

I gave him a shawl. He insisted on another one and started to argue when I refused. Seeing the crowd assemble, I quickly pulled out another of the shawls and handed it to him. One of the passers-by tried to distract him with stories of strangers moving around the area. Just as the driver turned and asked for my whereabouts, I threw my heap of shawls on the road and jumped out right after. I picked them up and dragged myself towards the embankment and sat there for what seemed like hours, clutching the shawls close to me. Nothing distracted me, not even the vacant expanse of Café Srinagar, situated right at the Bandh…or the aging chinar trees, the vacant chairs and the scattered leaves around the expanse. A solitary figure claiming to be the proprietor somewhat filled the vacuum. I sat outside Café Srinagar and munched on a ginger biscuit, which he said he had baked himself. 'Bake them myself, try them,' as he ventured forth to attempt to give me the recipe—of a strangely unbalanced combination of gingerly sugar amidst heaps of flour paste and, of course, that essential ingredient, saffron.

Surprisingly, there were no waiters, no chefs, no cashier, none of those ingredients to pinpoint at the silence of sorts. And then, quite surprisingly, even he suddenly disappeared! There were sudden cries of a crackdown and he'd run about haphazardly to join the lengthening row of hunched men and boys.

Rattled, I took a complete detour, bypassing the closed shopping complex, walking to the Dal Gate, further along the rows of shikaras lying stranded along the Jhelum—a river flowing through the heart of the Srinagar city with houses right till its embankments. The Hanji women had looked about hopelessly in the midst of settling those untidy scarves thrown about their heaving chests, clutching their fair-skinned children's hands.

Weary and worn out, I walked back to the Bandh—heading straight towards the café.

Once again, I sat staring at the vacancy, at the garden where the chinar trees sprouted rather effortlessly as though turbulence had to be taken in stride. I stared at those buildings standing absolutely still on the strength of mortar and bricks, without the support of any man or woman. I looked at that shuttered-down bank, those photo studios, that row of baked-down bakeries, that Ladakhi jewellery shop next to the handicraft store. Each one shut or semi-shut. Those boards with quaint names and surnames still hanging in their designated places. A man with a makeshift table-stand sat hunched in front of some hand-painted lamps and shades, but he seemed to be selling them more to himself, for there was no one else around. The length and breadth of the inner lane lay occupied with secure forms on the march. Each equipped with a gun. Not too sure to shoot point-blank or in the air, relaying and signalling.

Operation crackdown. Men and boys stood hunched all along the road. Also standing was that middle-aged proprietor of that café who had earlier stood right beside me, explaining his ginger cookie recipe.

Weighed down with the weight of the leftover shawls, I slumped near the man who was sitting hunched before a varied array of lamps. I didn't have the energy to speak so I pointed—towards no one in particular, perhaps those broken ends of that embankment.

He turned. And with a near upheaval writ large on his face, he let loose words and sentences—none of which could be put together. He stopped. And turned back, gazing at my face from a different angle. He looked accusingly, and more than that, suspiciously at me, at what I was doing there besides selling shawls in the midst of crackdown cries. He looked at me disgustedly. 'A woman selling shawls! You outsider! Here with our shawls! What's going on? You non-Kashmiris are ruining us!' When I asked whether he'd been exempted from that crackdown call, he countered, 'Me no rebel! A tourist guide can't rebel! Who can rebel without any legs? My legs were blasted off in Pahalgam… Nobody rebels here. One tried and there he sits in that dunga. He'd dared. Hounded he was, rounded up his collection. He used to roam all over your Hindustan. Now he sits in that dunga alone. But he's a rebel all right!'

'He…sells shawls?'

'No, no shawls.'

'No shawls! Then what? What collection?'

'Ask him…go to his dunga! That one… there! The one with that board.'

Chapter 2

I went in.

Into that dunga. Lying close to the embankment with a board that said 'My Getaway'.

No, he was not the shawl-seller I was looking for.

Yet I stood there staring. The low-roofed, oversized boat had books and newspapers piled up in heaps across its wooden floors, amidst cushions of all shapes and sizes sprawled all over. Right till the open space, from where stood out the embankment and the exteriors of the whole row of adjoining dungas.

I took one step forward and then another two backward. The wooden floor creaked wretchedly...as though it was sinking right into the deep waters. But he didn't bother to look back. He sat there looking straight ahead with a fierce intensity. Not at me, but at those dungas lined up, at those men and women going in and out of them, going up and down that haphazard path leading to the embankment. Unnamed and unmanned, these dungas were like the poor cousins of the famous houseboats of the Dal Lake, for though the houseboats occupied the prime waters, these followed much later when the Dal merged into the Jhelum.

And when he'd finally turned, there were none of those utterances asking about the mundane basics. His intense eyes looked tense, his confused emotions playing havoc. A strange sense of grief loomed large on his crestfallen face. Not a typically Kashmiri face. Definitely sunburnt. In fact, it was the intensity in his eyes that was his personality. A look that was strong enough to clasp. As though those two were going right into muscles and bones and flesh and intestines, right into, well inside.

He continued to mutter. As though he was kicking away his frustrations. He stamped a fleeing beetle. Crushed an escaping one. Flattened a mosquito on his frail chest till it spat his own blood before it flew away to squat on mine…then flew away further. The monotony was suddenly broken. It was a strained commentary, along a stranger strain as he suddenly let loose words. He spoke of rumours of the impending segmentations. Of places and people and pens. And with that, of even the verse, of those bygone historical imprints.

I tried to make sense of what he was saying. Those words—those long-winding sentences haven't quite faded even now. Each one of them coming through from some haze. Finally, he asked, 'Selling? You selling shawls? Can't buy...can't!'

'No seller...these shawls belong to that shawl-wallah. I'm searching for him.'

'You're not from here. You're an outsider. Which state have you been thrown out of? Are you seeking refuge? Or have you been uprooted?'

His words made little sense. I tried to move out of the wooden structure, but his gaze didn't allow me to. There was another outburst. 'You're shocked or what? That's the way I talk...' He carried on, 'Don't ask me too much. Meer is my name. Nothing more to tell you. Don't ask about my wife! It was a mismatch right from the beginning—my marriage...it was a mismanaged attempt to manage the mean mechanics of it all. We just about mated; it was masturbation with another woman's face hovering over mine. Bitch! No, don't ask about my life or wife like these middle-class rascals do. She lies elsewhere. I made it very clear, I want my own life. It's these men and women around me who are making my life hell. Can't move to any of those new colonies where today's moneyed people move around with their money. No, not one of them big-sized ones down there, but with that money making up for all those impotent moves, climbs...'

'What are you saying? I don't understand. Am just looking for a shawl-seller.'

'Who's selling what? Everything's seized...there is police everywhere.'

'Police? Here?'

'All over! All over! In all forms and shapes...even that legless man is theirs. He had taken Israelis to Pahalgam...' His eyes fell on the shawls. 'You're selling our shawls?'

'I'm no seller of shawls!'

'I'm no buyer either!'

'I'm looking for this other person...that shawl-wallah who sold them in my town, and his sons killed and my...'

'Where's his shop?'

'Shop? He doesn't have one. He used to go from town to town selling them. He'd left his sons with us but they were killed when our home was attacked.'

'Here?'

'Not here. I'm not from here. In Uttar Pradesh...our home is in a town you wouldn't know.'

'Which town? Pogroms happening, not in a set place but...'

'Bareilly.'

'Two Bareillys—one political and the other...'

'Raebareli is different. I'm from Baans Bareilly where...'

'Where two days back the Muslim mohallas got wiped clean, rioting and...'

'You know?'

'I read the newspaper...our Urdu akhbaars, not your Hindustani newspapers...know what's happening all over, know the politics of your towns. Who're you running from? Your police?'

'Occupied lies my home, those orchards, the bakery...

my father and brother killed, those Kashmiri boys killed and…I'm running for safety.'

'Killings on all over…no one gives any importance to death anymore. People come and go…it's those who are alive, who are on the run seeking refuge to be kept alive.'

Alive, he kept me. Alive and agile I was with him.

All those months…

At a stretch.

※

And now as I go crawling in this lock-up, those images hover around me. On his not-so-typically Kashmiri face. The fierce intensity in his eyes, strong enough to clasp me tight. Clasping my form with a maddening fury of severe want. All contained in those two eyes of his.

He'd transported me all over Srinagar city and its outskirts without actually moving even an inch. Taking me all over through a running commentary…a heady flow of words. Dastangoi of an amazing sort. It was those words and more words and slow, haunting descriptions of places and people that kept me alive. Taking me from one day to the next.

He near-halted any suggestions that he take me to the places he'd given me commentaries on. No, not even towards the lake, though unabated, he'd go about drawing out its three little-known segments. The Dal. Making me chant those descriptions till I was quite aware that there were actually three distinct layers to the lake.

For a stretch, I didn't step out of this wooden shelter, in fear of being questioned or counter-questioned. Not even to the local market along the embankment. It was shut half the time because of those ongoing shutdowns and then there was nothing to buy or sell. Ample haqsaag growing in the backyard to be pulled out and readied to be boiled in salt water. For a change, potatoes! No great food bandobast… no, none of those kilos of muttons that the Valley cuisine spreads are famed for…just his talks as he'd sit back, leaning on that mound of cushions, explaining impossibilities, coming up with complexities.

For hours we would sit, holding hands, and just talk… where he would tell me of those sexual encounters he'd had in those days he'd moved around along the coasts, around towns and cities. 'No, no boys ever…that's the one thing I haven't ever indulged in,' he'd say. He'd detail his other dislikes—killings and chopping and cutting sessions topped the list. He'd exclaim, 'No fleshy chunks for me! No slitting of throats!'

Sitting huddled in that rundown condition, he looked a misfit, not really fitting into this lower middle class set. Surviving, sitting stuffed in those lined-up boats stranded alongside.

Even now, as I open and close my eyes in quick succession, images of those chinars standing tall and stately not too far from that embankment come before me. More images keep resurfacing, refusing to slip by. Of freshly slaughtered goats along the embankment, together with the images of the dirt-embedded nails of those terror-stricken animals. I shake my head, hoping that this exercise would scatter some of those images. But they are unmoving. Determined to hover around, as though those imploring sounds were still forcing their way out of those partially slit throats of goats tied outside the row of dungas along that embankment, with Meer protesting that he could no longer witness the sight... Amidst horrifying sounds, blood had flowed out through those slit throats. Meer rushed into the dilapidated interiors.

Turned his back on them.

Turned to face me. As he held me for the first time. All through those earlier days it was only through his eyes that he made heady intrusions... He preferred to just snuggle. He didn't use sex as one of those near-confirmed escapist tools. It was always his large, well-set eyes taking the trouble of making love, as they would bore into me.

But that afternoon he had actually grasped me with want. Touched and retouched my small breasts, while offloading a commentary of sorts—of what diverse roles breasts play—beating of chests to pulling up of the chest, to suckle, to beckon, to attract. He'd carried on and on. I knew that my breasts had always been somewhat underdeveloped, but right now they looked as though they were under a strain of a peculiar kind. Secreting a series of desires, crawling...continuing to make way.

That afternoon Meer made love to me in that full-throated way. His eyes always darted here and there, without focusing on anything in particular. Till I found them focused on my teeth, as they stood out against my lower lip.

'These two…no, no, not your teats, your teeth…these front ones make me restless.'

'But they're so big and ugly…one's broken, stitched up, broke while climbing that tree and…'

'Don't know what can trigger off!' And with that his mouth was on mine, his teeth knocking against mine. Nothing stopped the fury with which he began biting, like a rabbit nibbling at my flesh. Not even sparing my long tresses. No, I did not need to be Alice in Wonderland to have known how rabbits bite and play and nibble and go on nibbling.

Lying on that wooden dunga floor with little space to roll about, he had caught my body. His face churned in untold emotions as he unhooked my brassiere. His hands on his penis. Taking it along, placing it haphazardly on my breasts, my stomach, then going further down.

Those images spread all around me—he rubbing his lips against mine. Pulling me back, grasping my breasts, sweeping aside the intruding hair. Running his fingers through my tresses, he positioned his legs to enter me. Then, no further releases or intrusions of any kind, in accordance with the rationed availability in these curfewed times.

Images hover around me as though I am still lying beside Meer who is holding my hand with a grip of the untold kind. My long strands were hidden under the shawl, and then no longer as Meer tilted his head, screwing up his nose, complaining that my hair smelt of raw eggs—with which I'd washed it just the night before.

I stretch out those details of him touching me here and there, right through that afternoon, peaking only around dusk. Getting his face right along my neck, rubbing along it as his fingers got going till he pulled them away to enter in that full-bloated way. Filling me up so very totally. But then withdrawing suddenly as though hit by some sort of realization. 'No…not at this age. I shouldn't do this…'

'What's age got to do with it?'

'You wouldn't understand…your wants are different, you're young…I'm getting a sinking feeling.'

'Sinking feeling? Why?'

'In my heart.'

'There's nobody around.'

'I'm not bothered about this lot! It's just that I cannot manage anymore. Done too much earlier. All those years…'

'With many?' I asked.

'I'm not a rogue. It's women who followed me and that woman…'

'Your wife?'

'Leave her out…we led a different life, moved about in your towns…even in your town and those others…now nothing's safe for us—we Kashmiris are all suspects in your Hindustan!'

Slight disruptions as he groped my front teeth.

Knocking his against mine. Till I started groping too. Pulling him towards me, my hands moving about beyond his stomach. Till his hands caught mine somewhere in between. As though they were halting their movement.

※

The memories suddenly stop. I bang my head on the concrete wall, trying to reactivate them. That image of Meer unleashing himself over my stomach before finding his way below, remaining stuck there for what seemed a long stretch. Till he'd all so very suddenly flung himself off…so very suddenly that I'd felt he'd hurt his stooping back. He looked as rattled by this sudden change, murmuring that no child should be conceived. I sat up. Unnerved. What if I conceived in this tight wooden structure, which had little space for human structures to move around? And that too with no nikahnama in hand? Wouldn't I get stoned to death, lashes leashed and unleashed in a hundred different ways? I think it was the first time in those months that we'd sat separately, as far from each other as we possibly could in that tight space. He didn't even look my way. Just sat there, brooding. That image holds out for a long time—looking forlorn, shaking his head in some sort of deep distrust, muttering that the people around would not let him survive and there was no other place he could flee to.

There was no place for me to flee to either, but that made little difference to that disturbed look in his eyes. He'd walked out hunched and returned armed with a pack of cigarettes. He seemed no novice as he lit the very first from the pack. Within an hour the empty carton was flung into those waters and settled, he lay on the cushions. No longer quiet. Throwing at me, rather recklessly, one query after another. What would happen if I conceived? Would I run away from there? From there to where? Where could I take the child? What would I tell those men and women stuffed next door once my stomach showed telltale signs?

I'd yelled and screamed hysterically. Screaming at him in one of my worst possible outbursts. I slowly sank into a corner, crumpled…then looked around for him.

I saw his eyes darting around. He was sitting not too far. He had a worried look on his face. 'No Kashmiri man would have kept a fleeing stranger…that too a woman! No Kashmiri would have kept an outsider like this. You came here looking for some stupid shawl-seller and here you are now staying with me…staying on.'

I had stayed on. Later perforce as I missed my next menstrual flow…and the next. Little did I imagine even in my wildest nightmares that I would conceive in the midst of this chaos. Worried, as options kept tightening. Even the option of running away to Bareilly. The option of stepping out on the inner stretch closed, what with my stomach bloating by the day. The money situation deteriorated further as the periodicals did not pay Meer even those fifty bucks they used to, saying that he was churning out repetitive stuff.

I'd often spot him eyeing my stomach, but he never brought up the topic of marriage. Not even when I once made him feel my bloated form. Even that running-his-hand-on-my stomach was done more for formality than anything else. He sat as though detached, but then not really so. Feeling from an unfeeling distance, he sat still, seeming to be drowned in a heap of sorrows.

※

As my pregnancy peaked, he stood hunched, pointing to my stomach. 'This child…where'll he be born? Here? Or do you want to go back?'

'Go back where? To whom? For what?'

'You're with a Kashmiri. You're sure to be detained.' He looked about, helpless and agitated. 'Police…police all around.' Opened the two little windows to the boat. Even as they carried a stench-ridden breeze, along with his apprehensions. 'This child…what can you give him here?'

'You and your talks!'

'Not enough…nothing left in me!'

'Well, that's what's kept me going, these months…'

He pulled me towards him and held me tight. Then he moved back just as suddenly, as I sat breathless.

'Your place…go to your town.'

'Who's left?'

'Search for someone.'

'Search with not even a rupee and… come with me.'

'Can't get uprooted. You'll be safer there without me…'

'I'm petrified. I can't ever return there.'

'Petrified? What worse can happen?'

'Police chief and those RSS men dine together… Muslims live in ghettos, changing names, chopping surnames and…'

'It's not safe to be together…we're not married.'

'So marry…marry me…I want to be with you.'

'Marry you I can—four times or forty, but then stuck! No getting away, no running away.'

His eyes looked like they were sucked right in, his fears whirlpooling. He started muttering. No breaks for his emotional drink, chai. No breaks for that faraway look—towards the waters stretching out as always. No breaks to read aloud to me what miracles the Sufis did or could do.

Instead, he kept taking me backwards to Calcutta and further back to some backwaters of Orissa and even to the Avadhi belts…he'd even gone as far as to my abba's and amma's towns—Bareilly and Shahjahanpur.

Did Kashmiris go that far?

After all, 'Valleyed' they lived. Giving refuge but not really seeking one.

His neck swayed, narrations holding sway, from an event to a non-event. Pointing out that his father was invited to give talks on Sufism. Like dervishes they'd moved around in those heady circles till the police accused him of spreading Islam.

'I loved collecting rare books…took up supplying books

about my region to all the regions of this subcontinent... book lovers came running for my rare collection till I was ruined. I've seen these politicians from those close quarters. Politicians, all third raters. All liars! Those ministers... speech after speech...that's all they give! After which they go tearing into the unpadded breasts of those freshly slaughtered chickens. Nobody discusses the impending segmentation of the state to be bifurcated and tri-furcated.'

He'd touch and re-touch the few remaining books he had. 'My collection of rare books—ruined, because I didn't give in. Didn't want to give in! Why should I supply or sell books with mischievous facts and figures, with twists and slants to them? Those men of that top government institution wanted me to sell some new history of this place, wanted me to twist the facts, wanted me to supply lies about my state, my people. I didn't give in, so here I am!'

'But you're no politician!'

'That's why I've been ruined by them! That's why my rare books are gone! They told me to create a controversy about this and that. So much pressure on me, too many threats and what not! They wanted a cooked-up controversy. That minister's man actually told me to create a controversy about the structures here. Once before, Sir Walter Lawrence tried doing so; writing that the ground on which Jami Masjid stands was sacred to Buddhists and Hindus. But this is not true...some big error. A.H. Franck's *Tibetan Notes* declare that structure is the Bodo Masjid and not the Jami Masjid. You know, Franck wrote details of that

Bodo Masjid. It is located below the castle hill of Srinagar… There are pictures of Buddhist saints behind the whitewash on the walls. Thankfully, those facts prevailed!' Looking angry and restless. 'That bloody political creature wanted me to create havoc! Circulate bizarre theories and cooked-up contradictions! I didn't give in. I'm like this—ruined—because I didn't give in!'

'Why're you talking about all this? Why're you getting so worked up?'

'Seen destruction…too much deceit by these political brigades. Fingering us all. Even history not spared. Today you Hindustani Musalmaans take in all that's thrown against Aurangzeb. Didn't he say that a masjid can be rebuilt in a couple of years, but chinars take hundreds of years? Yet your historians make him out to be some sort of rogue. It takes seconds for sparks. Prefix Afghans, Bangladeshis, Pakistanis and see how quickly arrests are made, how people are tortured.'

Meer was different in just about everything. Though he seemed to detest his wife, he hated the idea of talaq. So he kept his wife and sons at some distance in another of those dungas on the Nageen Lake. He made sure that his dunga was out of bounds for them. I wasn't too sure that he'd been visiting them either. He rarely spoke of his wife except once in a while, when he said he was used by her. When I asked why he was continuing his marriage when it was mismatched from the very start, he said, 'Because she's run away from her clan. She wanted to get out of their clutches.

She couldn't get to marry the Hindu teacher from her town whom she was in love with, so I was the second best choice for her. I met her when I was in her town supplying books, but got saddled with her. Now I'm stuck with her. We rarely shared the same roof, room, floor or a bed, yet two sons were born! Don't ask how! I was desperate to get away from her... stuffed myself into this dunga.'

He even had an explanation about why more and more people were stuffing themselves into these nondescript boats. 'This maddening rush for dungas is for obscurity and anonymity. They are not like the seedy hotels where managers go scurrying around taking pains to jot down addresses and pin codes, then taking more pains to forward them to those men from the intelligence agencies who are looking for people.'

ॐ

He wasn't comfortable with people hanging around close to our dunga. He was always suspicious of people trying to get a foothold. At times a Bengali woman would linger around the embankment, looking somewhat lost and forlorn...I didn't quite realize that she was from the eastern or western coast till Meer pointed in her direction, making it abundantly clear that I shouldn't talk to her.

'That Bengali woman,' he'd say each time he spotted her, 'is dangerous. She has many in her grasp. She's always here as though she owns these waters, these boats, this place.'

I used to sit and wonder—strange for this woman to come all that way from West or East Bengal, moving about, perhaps copulating with someone here along one of the margs or meadows, labouring it out on this unknown terrain. But why would a Bengali, whether from this or that side of Bengal, come to this side of the country? Why here—thousands of kilometres away and with the police in the foreground doing little less but going about unearthing Bengalis as never before?

I would keep wondering, thinking of the Bengalis hovering around our Bareilly home too. Any blast, cracker or otherwise, and ten or twenty of these so-called Bangladeshis were thrown into those hellholes of my home town Bareilly. That young woman who'd briefly come to our home to wash clothes had tried to camouflage herself with a bindi and Hindu signs till she discovered that we were Muslims. She'd then reverted to her original name— Shakeela Bano! We were shocked as she told us her tale in that aangan—of how she and her siblings were hounded out of their jhuggis by the local police. Once, while oiling my hair, she told me how her mother used to oil her hair… and then detailed that in one of those anti-Bangla moves, her mother was arrested and deported. Her siblings and she got stuck here. 'This desh shouldn't have helped in the creation of our desh to treat us like beggars…actually worse than beggars. We're no beggars…my forefathers built ships in your Kashmir! Ships and boats they built! No, no tales but true things…ask anyone, they built Kashmiri wooden structures, those ships and boats...whatever you call them now. My grandfather's uncles had even travelled towards Kashmir. One returned, the other did not.'

That was several years ago, but none of those details derailed from my head. How I'd turned my face towards her, but by then she'd moved towards my mother's silver-coloured tresses. Her big round eyes had moved on and about in complete anger as I sat ridiculing her claims. And then one day she disappeared. Never ever to be seen again, never to return to wash those heaps of clothes or to collect the money for those days she'd washed our stained, smelly undergarments and more. My mother sent our cook looking for her in that row of jhuggis where she said she lived. He came back only to tell us that some digging was going on for an upcoming lofty structure and that these Banglas were indulging in terrorist activities, so hoods were thrown over their heads and they were whisked away. My mother had heaved a sigh of relief, probably indicating that a terrorist could no longer oil our hair. But my father had sat perturbed that entire day about the hounding by the political goons and land mafia dons. The two sets collaborating to push away Muslims or those with Muslim-sounding names and surnames. That fear of deep insecurity lurked in his eyes as he worried. About our home. About our security. About my brother and me. Both of us unmarried. Both of us in that marriageable age...well, according to those prevalent norms in the Avadhi belts of Uttar Pradesh, irrespective of one being in this or that community. Marrying not necessarily for love or making love, but to produce forms with flesh and bones, with a head and tail. Well-bloated sperms!

It was probably for this reason, with this heap of backgrounders, that whenever I'd catch a glimpse of this Bengali woman lingering around the embankment, I would be reminded of Shakeela Bano.

One day when I told Meer about Shakeela Bano, he got irritated and muttered, 'This woman going about probing, wants to collaborate with the locals in more than straight ways…I've seen through her games!' He said that he found her not just inquisitive but daring. 'Imagine—she's asking me for books on boats! Wanting to know this and that, as though she owns a fleet here! Her bloody jurrat to try to come near me with all those stale games! Don't let her in.'

※

Though I'd stayed with Meer for months at a stretch, I had interacted only with those living in the two dungas on the right and left of ours. And that too, only on a couple of occasions. In one lived Shahjahan Abdul Ahad, who'd once been a waza and now sat idle because those big fat weddings were no longer there. He lay around, his eyes staring vacantly at those big rounded degchis he used to cook in, his hands busy slaughtering goats for several others stuffed in that row of boats. Meer would keep arguing with him, telling him that he couldn't see those slaughters. I have a distinct image of the day Meer threw up seeing a bone jutting out of the mouth of that waza while cooking atop a twisted kerosene stove in his dunga… He kept throwing up amidst the undertones of the lurking fears of getting roasted. 'Gutted boats can be rebuilt, but if one of the encircling chinars burn, it would take another hundred years for them to rise again.'

Again, as almost always, dragging in more, repeating those historic inputs. 'Badshah Aurangzeb had sunk into depression when the chinars got burnt along with the Jami Masjid. He was not as bothered about the burnt structure as he was about the trees…yet, there's all this propaganda against him.' Cynically, he'd quipped, 'It's not difficult to hire five people to write ten history books with biased accounts!'

Meer had drowned any further sessions of throwing up or delving deep down. Even the session of mixing boiled rice in some leftover curd, which he'd fetched from the shelves that lay overwhelmed by heaps of unwashed ware, to be further overwhelmed by some constant chatter coming from the adjoining dunga.

Ahad, unperturbed by Meer's long and short lectures on the virtues of vegetarianism, continued to be readily available to slaughter, till of course, the day he decided to go back to his native place Sopore. No, he didn't quite run away, nor was he hounded out. He just moved back.

Crawling, with my stomach rumbling and rattling, I recall the day I'd lain hungry on the bare wooden floor. Meer had looked into the empty bowls and then towards that waza Ahad's dunga. Maybe he was cooking something, as there was smoke coming out of his dunga. Meer walked out of the dunga and returned the very next minute. I sat up startled as I saw him back so soon. He had with him over half a dozen hens in a handmade sort of cage and a bag full of stale-looking vegetables. He handed them to me, together with the news that the waza was leaving for his village in Sopore. He'd barely sat down when the waza turned up, armed with more stuff. When he suddenly saw my bloated form, without that thick chaddar or that heavy embroidered shawl that I usually kept myself covered with, he was so shocked that he sat down almost immediately. He didn't, or rather couldn't, utter a word. He just stared. Not at me or Meer but towards the unmoving waters. Then towards the pale sky. Asked if we would shift with him to his village, set amidst apple orchards. He said he would look after the child and there'd be enough apples, if nothing else, to feed on.

Before he could add anything more, Meer shook his head. 'No more shifting for me. I've been hounded from one city to the other. This is my place and nobody can hound me from here.'

And with waza Ahad vacating that dunga, the only other person I could interact with was the half-widow Shagufta and her son Osama. She lived as though someone had pushed her into an oblivion of sorts right into the backwaters, till that evening when we—she and I—had spoken at some substantial length, only once, on that haphazard way that led to our dungas. I remember I had ventured out somewhat that one evening and stood on that little patch. Just about then, we noticed a small group moving towards the third dunga in that row, to be followed by an unending round of luggage being taken out and then taken in. Distracted by this sudden movement, I came near where Shagufta stood with near-dripping clothes clasped in her arms. I smiled weakly at her, looking for some sort of a reciprocation, before she burst out in Kashmiri. Sensing my blank look, she quickly changed into a mix of Urdu and Kashmiri as she uttered in a high-pitched voice between throwing about withered phirans on the grass, 'You from where? You here searching for someone? A missing brother or father or son?' More clothes…along with more words, many more details—the way her husband had been picked up for questioning and never, ever came back. She rattled off the names of police stations and detention centres, places she'd gone looking for him. Unable to trace him, she'd joined ranks with the hundreds of half-widows surviving in and around this Valley. After she'd sold off their one-roomed home downtown and her husband's scooter rickshaw, she tucked herself into this rented wooden structure with her schoolgoing son, while running around pleading to the ministers and visiting human rights delegations. She'd sat in protest meets for the disappeared, travelling right till New Delhi to lodge complaints with human rights set-ups, little realizing that her name would then be fitted in that dreaded list of those local vocals who'd dared to speak out as much as their vocal chords could carry through.

She kept up her monologue till I finally broke the monotony by asking whether her fears had been compounded or exaggerated. Even now I can visualize the expressions changing on her pale face, in her eyes—ranging from frightful bewilderment to absolute anger. Her eyes almost bulged out of their sockets as she took five steps forward towards me—her bosom next to mine, her lips hanging close to my ear. 'Can't you see? Can't you tell what's going on! These men just got into that dunga. They're from CID…Haneefa told me this…yes, she's selling eggs there… but Rafeeqa says it's the governor janaab himself, says he grew a beard and stayed in a masjid but when information leaked that those Amreekans will bomb the place, he went running all the way to his bhavan where all these laat sahibs live sheltered and in safety!'

Her lips had intensified their movement. 'So many getting picked up by these creatures. Don't know what's going to happen. Even children not spared, rounded up, to be dragged for questioning! You've seen my son—he's so small but he knows what's going on. Just six years old when these wretches picked up his father. All he's seen are searches and more searches and those crackdowns. I want my husband back…but let's see what Allah wants.'

On that note she rushed up another ten steps as she saw her young son Osama returning from that school across the main road.

Those images of her son Osama take over. He was a young child but unlike other children, he rarely ventured out, except to that nearby school. Then not even that. He was picked up the very next night—that night when we heard loud cries coming from that half-widow Shagufta's dunga. Those cries ruptured the night. Darkened lay the stretch. Bloodied lay the waters with that half-widow's lifeless form. To add that additional reddish tinge to the flow, overflowing with contributory blood from those others ripped apart.

Before we could make out how very bloodied they lay or where exactly her floating form was—was it first turned upside down and then thrown in—curfew was clamped amidst cries of a crackdown. And with that the security forms forced their way into the other dungas along the embankment.

I'd placed my bony fingers on my bloated stomach, naïvely trying to provide protection for my child lying within me. Apprehensive that we'd be next on their long list, I clutched Meer, pleading that we move out.

'Where to? Towards the ziarats and dargahs? Towards the masjid along the embankment? Towards those yateemkhanas? Where?' He sat there unmoving, looking tense. He shook his head in dismal motions. 'Searches! Police around…along the embankment, barging in.'

I shut my eyes, as though that alone would halt the flow of images, spread out as never before, flitting from one to the next: from that half-widow's form to those full-fledged widows staring out vacantly from those far-flung dungas. Till search parties unleashed their activities at an alarming pace. Till the entire area was cordoned off, checking on owners and ownership. Till Meer was made to stand hunched, lined up along with the rest of the others. Till queries and doubts were raised about names, surnames and much more. Till his pleas were vehemently vetoed by many of the inspectors solely in charge of checking and rechecking. Those kicks resounding as he raised his head. To mutter and re-mutter. Getting stuck and stammering in a wild fashion. They'd pulled him towards a row of bodies—already semi-deadened by baton wounds, lying crumpled on the embankment.

I flung my hands about in desperation. I'd always done this—even in junior school when I'd be late for the bus or hadn't quite completed my homework or when the bus passed by my stop after waiting for a while for me. That night, I sat banging my hands on the dunga's wooden floor. Crying. Crying for Meer. Crying for the newborn pushed and pulled out of my pelvic interiors. My legs moved about on their own accord—they continued doing so even when I was pushed into the van to be driven back to home territory by the special cell men calling themselves Tearing Tigers—tearing through those broken roads of Uttar Pradesh. Till the van halted at the outer municipal limits of Bareilly.

No further…no road ahead.

※

No, not to my father's kothi. That had been taken over by the establishment for their freshly set-up Anti-Terror department, duly named The Terror Tower.

I was shoved into the refugee camps set up on the outskirts of Bareilly town for those ruined in the riots. The officials manning these camps told visiting political delegates that these were homes for rescued Musalmaan women.

This was where, every long night, I tried to throttle myself with a heap of unsettling questions. Why didn't I fight back? Why didn't I stay put to counter those moves to throw me out of the Valley? Why did I let them throw me into the van? Was I scared that they'd clamp murderous labels on my stained shalwar if I didn't adhere to their orders? Why didn't I run from jail to jail, from one interrogation centre to another, looking for the man who'd made love to me first with his eyes, then in more ways than one? Why didn't I fight it out? Was I scared of fake charges being thrown at me? Was I scared of being made to sit like a deadened sardine along with the hundreds of other forms stuffed in the unwanted category, dumped to rot amidst the many others rotting away?

Those images of the dunga didn't leave me even for a minute, all those days and long nights at the refugee camp. I felt as though I was still gazing at the unmoving waters of the river, at the chinars standing tall, at the side wicker gate leading to the embankment on one side and lane connecting it to the other end. As though I was actually still there… clasped not in that cold covering, but in the warmth of Meer's unmoving gaze. Nothing really coming in the way, not even the news that hundreds were fleeing from the very city which I was readying to near. I was desperate to be with him and my child.

I brushed aside those conflicting voices inflicting fear on my already fragile form. Grabbed that measly compensation sum for my ancestral home, now in the clutches of the state. The sum, just about enough to buy a rail and an air ticket. The train taking me from the confines of the Bareilly refugee camps to New Delhi. The plane taking me further ahead to Srinagar.

Returning to Srinagar once again, after so many long months, in the autumn of 1994…determined to trace Meer and my child.

Chapter 3

Hundreds fleeing the Valley overnight, becoming refugees in their own land. Moving away from one sector to the next... Those stranded in their own dwellings and dungas across the Jhelum were sitting amidst strange fears and uncertainties brought about by political complexities. The Muslim Kashmiris could not move beyond the Jawahar Tunnel—the exit point that had seen hundreds of Kashmiri Pundits fleeing from the so-called Paradise. Towards the mainland...

It was in the midst of this turbulence in the autumn of 1994 that I reached Srinagar. The second time... The stretch outside the airport was overburdened with several in uniform. Very few civilians and even fewer taxi drivers hanging around looking for customers. One came near me as though he couldn't bear to be overshadowed by the heavily laden firing bandobast.

I ignored him, looking about for an autorickshaw or a bus. His smirk was enough to suggest that it would be a folly to think that they'd be parked in this stretch of the severely guarded airport.

Flinging that lone bag on the backseat of the taxi, I looked out of the window as we moved. Army convoys moving about with much urgency, matching the urgency within me. Perhaps also matching the driver's as he stretched his neck backwards and forwards to unleash a wildly worded commentary of sorts. He had a strange rebellious look that couldn't contain nor conceal his unease. He blurted out in somewhat reasonably fluent English, 'Curfew…jammed…curfew till Pampar and…'

'Till Pampore?'

'Hukumat's rule—worse than Hitler's. Yesterday's firing left more than a dozen dead…shot in their heads…business over…only business of killing, killings, firings going on. Let me drive quickly otherwise these Biharis will kick… shoot… You want to go where? Your pass…curfew pass with…'

He turned to look at me, sensing that I was taken aback. 'No pass…no passing through city. Know what's happening here? Your radio, your televisions, all blaring that…'

He slammed on the brakes rather suddenly and the car screeched to a stop.

It was a check post. To check limbs—mine, his and the vehicle's. And looking for that pass, to let us pass.

His frayed collar gave away as their secure fingers moved up and down his body. Their gaze shifted like a semi-rusted pendulum to me. They flung him back on the seat, gesturing that he reverse. 'No going ahead…sit somewhere in airport. Curfew ahead,' they said curtly.

I took my face close to his back to sheepishly whisper to him to drop me off anywhere, but out of there.

'Taking you there,' he said.

'No, not to the airport but….'

'Taxi is not mine…have to give it back before the bypass. You can telephone someone. I cannot drive any further into the city. Get someone,' he said to me urgently.

He was shocked at my bewildered expression.

'Nobody? Why're you here then?' He glared into the mirror, adjusting it till he could meet my eye. He couldn't have been more than in his mid–twenties, although he looked older. He strained to think and then said wearily, 'One kilometre from this turn, depends on…'

'On what?' I sound desperate.

'Why ask so much?' He re-adjusted the mirror and zipped down the road till a roundabout. Rows of rundown shops with their shutters down lined the right side of the road. A small group of young boys standing nearby stopped what they were doing as the rattling ambassador halted right beside them. He rushed out of the taxi and was back within a minute, clutching a pack of cigarettes firmly, as if it would be pulled out of his grasp. He shook his head disgustedly. 'No, not here…'

'Then?'

'I'll take you to some discarded old boat or…'

'No…just…' I hesitated, not knowing what to say. My mind was muddled. I couldn't think.

'You alone? Someone more coming?' he asked, rather too impatiently. He looked at me in a strange way. This time not via the mirror but directly. Too directly. 'Foreigners with no pass want old rooms or old boats or…' He pulled out an ID card and flashed it into my face almost in a fit of frenzy. 'ID card, my life saviour, otherwise my neck twisted. These jaanwars don't even wash hands. You like me or them?' he made a crude gesture of his neck being twisted.

'You're…what?'

'Musalmaan, Sunni. You?'

'You tell me?' I asked quite brazenly as I thrust my face and neck out of the window, away from his glare. Away from any more questions. Away from any connections he could possibly concoct. Bringing a temporary halt to the conversation.

Then again.

'You without pass! You not from here? Speak Kashmiri?'

I didn't bother to answer.

He waited discreetly for an answer, then seemingly gave up, veering the conversation to something else.

'This road going to bypass. Will drop you there.'

'There! Then…'

'Then do what you want. Go where you have to.'

'Till where?'

'Till nowhere! No one can roam around because the place is occupied.'

'Occupied? How?'

'Not just by the police and politicians, but lingering memories, suffocating all of us! My father said memories kill…nothing else kills but only memories!'

'Memories? Memories of what?'

'Asking too much now. No more. Crossing is here but just see…crackdown is on there and everywhere.'

Standing outside was a haphazard row of hunched men. Several young boys, in all probability their sons, squatting insecurely at some distance. Pulling out weeds and throwing about insecure looks. At no one in particular. And yet at just about anyone. I imagined how I'd stand hunched just like the others, waiting endlessly.

'Cannot go anymore. You landing when these KPs running.'

'Pandits?'

'Out of this hell. Not stuck like us. You have work here? You not like us. You not from here?' He stared at me unashamedly. Seeming to take pains to study my face—his glare moving quickly from my nose to my eyes and my mouth. He blurted out, 'Not sure who's who nowadays.'

'Who?'

'This hukumat has hundreds of agency people—informers who keep a watch on us. Day and night.' He continued to glare at me. 'We have reached. Get out now. Here. Walk that side in that lane.' He pointed to the lane at the far end of road. I pulled the ends of my chaddar closer but the strong breeze came in the way.

I adjusted my spectacles. 'Whose homes? Who lives here?'

'No one. The Pandits have gone. We are the ones that got left behind. We cannot go to your India and neither can we go the other way. The buses can ply from here to Muzaffarabad, but not our bodies.'

'But...'

'What do you want?'

'Leave me near the town,' I told him firmly.

'Can't you see there's a crackdown?' he snapped as we walked towards that inner lane.

I followed him in the strange quiet. From the outer lane to the by-lane. To another of those clusters. The dwellings just about standing, with not a single form to be spotted anywhere. The lane was absolutely deserted.

'All caught in the crackdown or what?' I asked.

'This is where the Pandits lived. Those crackdowns are for us. To crack our skulls.'

The burnt and semi-burnt darkened homes came into view, one after another. A forewarning of a sort. Another row of those semi-burnt vacant homes loomed before me. We passed a school. The empty school compound made it impossible to imagine children playing or sitting around with their books and tiffin boxes. The vacancy spread—through the dangling twisted iron gate into another weed-infested compound, overflowing with garbage and strange piles of rot.

Looking about wearily, he and I walked cautiously right

till the end of this garbage-riddled expanse. More buildings and some human forms, but as though deadened by the constant onslaught. Semi-tiered structures stood agape. Ripe enough to tell a story yet decayed with deep cracks showing. Sharp-featured faces frowning. Forms hunching. Fear gnawing deep, frustration rising high. Poverty had consumed several of those standing about blankly. Many had hurriedly shifted base, leaving their homes, trying to deal with the insecurity left unchecked by the political administrators. Unaware that securities unleashed by these very guarantors would come in the way. No one quite sure whether they were to be quite simply stacked in those missing slots, in the undertrial list or left to simply wallow in the many camps set up here and there. Heavily banking on the fact that roots—human or otherwise—hurriedly pulled out and thrown asunder in some sort of a frenzy, find it hard to strike again. Wilting. Dying. Getting dumped. In nondescript graves. Freshly dug. Or quite simply, reduced to ashes, leaving little scope for an uprising.

Stumbling along, we suddenly found ourselves before a gaping grave. Open and wide. Ready and waiting. Desperate to swallow yet another frame. Impatient to tuck in some more bones and fleshy reserves. Almost falling into the scooped-out expanse was a boyish-looking man digging with his bare hands. He looked totally rattled, backing a few inches away from the scooped expanse, as though this opening was relaying reminders of a woman's opening. Wanting yet awaiting.

As we neared the young man, the taxi driver spoke. It was more of a mutter under his breath, 'You digging for what? More bodies in this curfew? Paagalpan! Madness!' Muttered more, 'Move, run from here. Nothing safe here.'

'Check whether...'

'Check what?'

'Police and...'

'All around.'

'Can't run. Where to go?'

'But you're carrying this body...'

'I'll take it there right in front of them.'

'They'll pull it apart!'

'Whatever remains of it.'

Suddenly giving each other accusing looks, and throwing some towards me, the driver whispered, 'My brother Shukoh, he buries the dead. You outsiders kill and we cover your sins.'

'And you?' I asked.

'I am Aurangzeb. Are you here to see us dying?'

'Stop it!' I suddenly realized that I was sitting atop a row of graves. 'There's a bone sticking out!' I yelled, trembling. Another bone touched my ankle. Fear gripped me. I was trembling. I had trembled this way just once before—when I was caned in junior school for pointing at the missing buttons on the shorts of a small boy who sat beside me.

I'd shouted rather blatantly, 'Ma'am, there's a lizard in his shorts!' As the rest of the class gathered around him to see how he was surviving with the reptile clinging to him, he shocked them by stating rather matter of factly that it was no reptile, but his own penis! 'My own thing,' he'd gone on and on confidently till he, together with his 'thing', were reduced to a mere little crumpled mess. The teacher, popularly called Moral Science ma'am, not having seen one in her long stretch of spinsterhood, couldn't recover from this pronouncement. She dragged us both to the principal's room. The principal, a spinster too, strained to look and re-look at the offending sight and then caned him till his organ turned numb like a cold-blooded reptile in hibernation. She pulled me by my untidy plaits and threw off my thick glasses. As though the simple exercise of not being equipped with spectacles could keep one away from such sights. And if that wasn't enough, she slapped me across the face with such a spate of energy that the set of braces saddled across my rabbit-like teeth rattled.

And this evening again, as I sat on a mound with bones jutting out of the freshly dug graves, I started trembling. I shifted my posture, looking around, staring at the graves. I felt certain that one of those bones was alive—kicking me, forcing me to move away. I couldn't kick it back, nor could I cry out in fright.

The younger of the two men began a commentary of sorts, 'Yet to bury this little child. The body's rotting. It will not stand the heat of another day. The hair stuck to the bloodied mass. Loose limbs falling apart and…' Placing the cloth back on the remains and removing some of the mud that had crept into his socks, the young man stood up wearily. 'Young…just some months old this little child… even been circumcised.'

Aurangzeb threw up. 'Stop it! I don't want to hear any more of these descriptions. Why carry these remains? Why get arrested?'

'It has to be buried…be given a decent burial because…'

'You think you are Mulla Muhsin Fani? Influenced by Bachi or what? Running around in this curfew like that treacherous subedar Zafar Khan Ahsan.'

'Enough of this!' He looked about helplessly at the row of graves. 'The dead have to be buried.'

'What if you're arrested?'

'Then what? What remains? There's nothing left. We're all lurking around in fear. Even the letters of the alphabet are mistaken for anti-national literature these days.'

'You wrote more verse.'

'It was for survival.'

'The dead don't read.'

'I'm alive. Still alive. These remains cannot be left for the vultures.'

'Where are you going? How far?'

'Obviously not going to Pari Mahal or Zeashta Devi Shrine.'

'There's curfew on right from Lal Chowk. There are crackdowns all over right up to Nowhatta Chowk.'

'See these bruises?'

'Where have you been? Crawling?'

'What else?'

'Throw them into the Jhelum. It takes in everything.'

There was a sudden silence. They glared at each other, realizing that they'd said too much and spoken much too blatantly in front of a stranger.

Aurangzeb penetrated the silence, with his eyes penetrating further, making inroads through my clothes into my bones and flesh.

'Shukoh buries, doesn't kill. He says the dead are not really dead, they're aware of what's happening around them,' he said by way of explanation.

I wanted to scream. Instead, my voice came out softly, 'Get me out of here.'

'Go back to where you landed. Are you here to meet someone, or is it something else?'

'To meet...'

'Who?'

'Don't know if he's still here.'

'A man?'

'Yes, a man...a man from here.'

'Your friend or...'

'I had lived with him, had a child.'

'You or he?'

'Ours...his and mine.'

'Here we're dying and you're rattling all this bloody rubbish!'

'But you asked and…'

'Can't you see my brother carrying these remains? Some baby's. I must return the taxi before a search party lands up here and…'

He looked about impatiently as his brother muttered, 'What about her? Take her along and drop her wherever she wants to go.'

'Without the pass?'

'Then?'

'Carry her…'

'Where! Going crawling…have to crawl along!'

'Crawl?' I asked in disbelief.

'Then stand here amidst these graves.'

'Take me away from here!'

'Then crawl. Like an animal. Like an animal, crawl on all fours for survival.'

Chapter 4

Shukoh and I sat still for a while before crawling. We bypassed stunted apple trees. Listless and barren, akin to a woman's form that has had its uterus and ovaries plucked out by gynecologists and their accomplices, the midwives.

An eerie spread, furthering...further. Around those margs or meadows where we saw none of those Gujjar groups with their bhairu herds. They seemed to have all systematically throttled themselves, sheepishly or aggressively, with handmade woolly loops. We passed several remains, hazy foot imprints, dried heaps of stale dung—enough to suggest that cattle had once passed this way before being overtaken by usurpers.

I crawled along with Shukoh, trying to keep pace as he clutched those remains close. With the shrubbery gaining ground, so did the nauseating smells. I crawled clumsily, trying to find the means to escape from that smell of rotting flesh. The smell, that I was under the illusion of leaving behind, resurfacing. Being pulled back. As if this stretch was nothing short of a road leading to a tannery with hides hanging from everywhere.

As a child I'd been to a tannery on the outer city limits of Kanpur. What I saw there left a deep impact on me. Nothing discreet. Hides hanging upside down. With the mind wandering, wondering—why just animal hides? Aren't live human forms hung upside down in prison hellholes, in municipality-run orphanages or in the midst of those asylum wards?

The stench of the rotting hides billowed around me, carrying forth a fresh installment of the nauseating smell, as though the hides had been set to boil in water that looked like it was pumped out of the municipal corporation's rundown reservoir.

All too suddenly, the words leapt out before I could clamp my mouth shut, 'Are there animals around here? Bears, langoors?'

Shukoh looked at me rather intently, just like his brother had done not more than a couple of hours ago, 'Your people are fleeing, but you are here. Why?'

'My people? Who?'

'Pandits!'

'Do I look like one? A Pandit, I mean?'

'Maybe. But…'

'Do I?'

He changed tracks. 'This is my place.'

'Then why crawl?' I asked angrily.

'To bury this.' He threw his shawl lookalike around his back. Almost hitting my face. I tried to move backwards but landed sideways instead on the boulders, bruising my elbow.

'Miles to go. This the other end.' He looked unapologetic.

'Can't see without my spectacles…I think I dropped them somewhere.'

'You've come this far for just what?' he asked, ignoring my comment.

'Looking for…'

Before I could finish my sentence, he butted in, 'Spectacles? Didn't see you wearing them.'

'How could you? You were digging and then…'

As I looked around, he reached out towards me. I shrank back as he quickly plucked my spectacles from within the folds of my chaddar. 'Spectacles, here!'

Then, in a stranger way, frowning at his own hands clutching the remains, 'Can't bury here. Even the slightest sound around these pillars erected during Ashoka's time will cause them to shoot to kill in this high security area. The new cantonment is not far but those men are at every turn and crossing with orders to shoot to kill.'

Words coming in way of the boulders, the bare mountain peaks, ruined remains of those erstwhile structures of those dynastic times down the tumbling terrain. He was stooped, looking pathetic with those remains still clutched to his chest.

'Bury these here...'

'No, not here.'

'Why?'

'Not safe!'

'What's wrong with you? Bury it!' I was getting impatient now.

'What?'

'You haven't buried them yet?'

'What?'

'These remains and...'

'And what?'

'Your wants!'

'Yours or mine?' His gaze tore through me. 'No identity card on you, yet you're here. But you're not from here. Our women don't go around like this shamelessly.' He spat out the words contemptuously.

'Dress code?'

'Yes, of course.'

'Don't follow blindly.'

'You are following me.'

'You're not moving. Like these remains, you are getting me stuck in these ruins.'

'But these are no ordinary ruins! Temples, dargahs and...'

'Temples? Here?'

'You know what Jehangir and Mirza Haider Dughlat

wrote about the temples of this place? Read *Tarikh-i-Rashidi* and you'll know. There are not one or two, but more than 150 temples here!'

'Where?'

'All around here but all gone now.'

'How? Destroyed?'

'Yes, down the years.'

'By whom? You all?'

'Us? No. Not by us…never by us. Destroyed by earthquakes and landslides. What else! Not like the way your Babri Masjid was brought down by those goons.'

'You know about that?' I was surprised.

'Yes I do. We all do. Know all about your political mafia who will do anything for power… Read our real history, read those true accounts. None of the twisted slanted versions…some useless writers blame Sikandar for temple destructions here but not true. Sikandar had even married a Hindu woman called Cricobha… You know, our people and their struggles are not like in your India and Pakistan. Don't want either and yet those talks. Throwing baits, all sorts of creatures sent here.' He looked angrily towards me and continued, 'You here for what? To fool around with these security creatures? Spare me—we're fighting battles with the hukumat for the last so many years. You wouldn't know about it.' He ended his monologue bitterly.

'Why did you get me this far then?' I asked.

'Police are circling these areas. Don't I know their third-class politics—they catch hold of even children and rape them,' he responded without looking up. Settling and resettling rather haphazardly that rattled-looking crumpled mess of a shawl on his shoulders, he threw a questioning look at my bag. 'No shawl?'

'No, just this chaddar and…'

'Chaddar! Talking of chaddars when I'm talking of shawls. Shawls are shawls!' He sat unmoving like an animal in the basic stage of labour. 'Our shawls are different; the weaves and patterns are different. During our badshahs' time, our shawls were presented to Napoleon Bonaparte. They were a craze all over the world. But now, stacks of them lie around unsold.'

I stared at him, at the shawl on him… The sound of gunshots at a distance made it impossible to continue crawling any further. We sat huddled amongst a pile of boulders as the sound of the moving convoy gained ground. Unmoving, his body next to mine. Pushing himself nearer, moving inches away from those heavy boulders. Closer, his skin rubbing rather too casually against mine. I felt his hands on my stooping back, withdrawing and then not so. Probably waiting for me to react or counter-react. His fingers moving and then moving along. I felt his fingers rubbing the length and breadth of my huddled back, even as I quite half-heartedly murmured, 'Stop it.'

'Can't run.'

'Is there no other way?'

'Run before they slap charges on you!' he said urgently.

'But I haven't done anything.'

'Who does anything? Charges are hurled at passers-by too.'

'But aren't you going ahead? Why?'

'Towards a hellhole! Either way I'm finished.'

'For what?'

'For being a post-graduate, yet digging holes. Let them destroy me. Let my bones and flesh lie knotted and clotted in these bursting graveyards. They cannot take any more dead forms. Too many graves.'

'I saw children play around those graves near the embankment when…'

'Saw? How?'

'Because I'm also a post-graduate.'

'But you're moving around like a third-rate woman. Now come closer to this rock. This side. Your shadow will give us away. Slide closer. Near me. Next to me.' He pulled me a few inches closer to him, his hand dangerously nearing my breasts. Pausing. Waiting for a reaction or a counter move. Sensing none, he pulled me close, touching my breasts. Slowly. Then with a terrifying intensity. I felt his teeth on my cheek. On my chin. Digging into my flesh. Throwing aside worries about a broken tooth, even with his teeth nearing mine. His teeth settling on mine…till I could sense mine rattling. Moving away from his grip, bringing in a distraction of sorts.

'Why bury?' I asked.

'What?'

'Bury.'

'Bury or worry?'

'The bodies...the dead.'

'Their eyes stare on, to haunt me for nights to come. My father's been turned into a butcher. Forced to slit throats. Says each time he slits those bhairus, their eyes look accusingly, asking for reasons for being put to death.'

'You're talking about goats?'

'Sheep, goats, our bhairus. Their eyes...forewarning us with that strange look.'

'Forewarning? You're married?'

'No.'

'No?'

'Marriage amidst bullets? My mother admitted into the ward...now pulled into a hellhole! My father can't cry or laugh, just glares at what he chops.'

'What?'

'Bhairu—for men and women.'

'You haven't been near a woman?'

'No. This is the only city in the world which has no lal mohalla!' he sneered.

'But so many sex scandals.'

'You outsiders creep in and throw us in the midst of these convoys.'

'But you've never...er, never neared even one, not even an animal?'

'This isn't your Vilayat or that devil's land Amreeka! Animals? They're to be eaten!'

'Isn't fucking a different way of devouring?'

'What? Fucking?'

He caught my face between his hands savagely. His teeth on my teeth. On my stomach. Nibbling. Biting. Clawing haphazardly with little coordination between his limbs, nervousness throwing them here and there maddeningly.

Clamping my mouth every now and then. Clasping me, throwing himself atop me. Pulling and pushing my breasts. Whispering, then mumbling something. A strange commentary. Along the strain of images of gaping graves resurfacing, the emptiness around us, he sneered at his own capabilities.

His fingers found a discreet way to my brassiere hook. Unhooking it, he let my heaving breasts tumble out. His fingers pulling at my nipples. Pampering them, then fiercely pulling them as beasts do. Pulling with unabated want. His fingers crawling rather haphazardly towards my stomach, to the thighs.

'Are you a weaver?'

He was taken aback. Looking about wildly again before settling back between those boulders, 'No...no, no weaving...reduced to just being a digger and delver and...'

He loosened the strings of the shalwar. His fingers nervously found their way inwards. Making inroads. Placing his hands tight on my mouth, my feeble voice coming through in a strange way like a second-hand, much fiddled-with vehicle finding its way through New Delhi's potholed roads. Stuffing his fingers into me...shoving them in further and further, till I could bear it no longer.

'Hurts. Please don't…'

'Shaadi hui? Married?'

'No.'

'But it's not the first time.'

'No, not the first time.'

'With whom?'

'With the man I was living with.'

'You doing all this without marriage? That's the worst gunah.'

'You?'

'No…never before. But wait, there's blood…see…'

'Menstrual.'

No counter cry, but like most men brimming with sheer practicality, he released himself on my stomach.

The sounds of a passing convoy intruded the moment, making a hue and cry about the peculiar release taking place. It ebbed into the wilderness, making further intrusive invasions into another terrain, leaving us staring at each other.

Back to reality. Slowly moving on, crawling ahead, leaving a bloody trail as we did. Crawling like animals on all fours. The shrubbery thinned out and we found a place to squat, his head squeezed between two boulders. He dragged me close to him and pushed me alongside the boulders. I lay unmoving, semi-stuck between the boulders. Muttering slowly but continuously, he began a strangely worded bizarre commentary on those images in his head—

of him squeezed between his mother's drooping breasts. His dried lips on the shrivelled nipples, he chewing on them. Craning his head out of that strange juxtaposition, but sitting still. Very still. Throwing up. One idea after another. Muttering again. Nothing left in him except ideas, tossed about effortlessly. If only he had joined the youth wing of one of the freshly floated offshoots of the right wing, he could have had some support. Or else got adopted by one of the farsighted schemes of the Great Alliance wherein his life would have been insured in exchange for the spread of terror tactics. Or better still, he could have changed his own name and that of his father and grandfather too. And with that, perhaps, he would have moved on. At least somewhat beyond the Tunnel.

Holding his organ as though it were just another long cut of a discarded intestine, he ripped apart his pyjamas, partially baring his thighs. He shook his head, hysterically heaping curses. 'Is this my end? Doing it over your breasts… am I impotent or what? If I pull and push these balls what'll be left for those Bihari bastards in the interrogation centre…bastards!'

He started as he saw me readying to crawl out once again. Not sure whether he should stop, follow or else hold me, he looked on, bewildered. Then not so. He started crawling. Over me. All over again. Till the gunshots took over.

He pulled me back to himself, putting his head on my chest, snuggling close. He rattled on non-stop, like he was seized by a series of frenzied fits.

'Once before, I was half-running, half-crawling through the freshly tilled land, down the slopes, reaching the barren hills. Taking refuge in one graveyard. My people with me as we'd lain close to those graves, very close to the bones and skeletons of those long dead,' he babbled on and on, raising his head and shrugging his shoulders, as though that simple exercise would shake off those images.

We looked across the wire fencing. It wouldn't be easy to crawl beyond the barbed wires along the semi-wilderness where the spring waters flowed.

'This isn't Chashme Shahi springs...it flows on the other side of the city near the Dal, cutting its way through terraced gardens laid out by the Mughal Emperor Shah Jahan.' He shrugged. 'Been to Chashme Shahi many times when Father still had some money left. I remember how he'd walk us to the lake...you know, in Kashmiri, dal means a lake, but in Tibetan it means still waters...I go by the Tibetan.'

'Your father a scholar?'

'He's different from the rest but never at rest...says the Sufis haven't died even though they've been buried... they wander around, transporting themselves from here to there in various garbs. Whenever he'd taken us to the Kas-i-Mah ruins, he looked about for them as though their souls were still lurking around in human forms...but that was years ago when we could move about somewhat freely... he'd always say there's something special about the Sufis. He made us read Mughal Emperor Jehangir's memoirs, those details to the simple Sufi ways. He read to us details of Abu'l Fazl meeting with Wahid sufi, who for thirty long years sat still in a corner gathering happiness on an old mat!'

'Your father knows all this? What about your mother?'

'These creatures call her foreigner! Foreigner!'

'British?'

'No, not a gora.'

'Bangladeshi?'

'No. Half Afghan.'

'Afghan?'

'Her memory's going. These days she just mumbles about those days in...'

'In Kabul?'

'No, not Kabul...anyway, what's left of it. Those dogs... came here suspecting her, us, each one of us...calling us foreigners. These RR men go running around with their dogs looking for Afghans! Afghans, Afghans, Afghans, they go around shouting, barging into homes, throwing open doors, jumping through windows... My mother sits staring into space, repeating incidents from the past, but who's around to listen to her? Father ran away from my mother... hates her Afghan connection. The two were never together. Been like two escapists in a state of perpetual confusion... what else to say!'

'Collaborating bodies.'

'Why talk this rubbish?'

'I was talking about...'

'You're talking stupid rubbish! Collaborations don't last. Don't know why she married him. They were totally mismatched. She was far ahead of her time. Till about five years back she was flinging things into a suitcase as though set to free herself.'

'From your father?'

'Don't know if it was from him or from here. But nothing's in one's control. Nothing at all! My father wanted to change the course of our lives only through books and facts…look where we've reached! Hounding and pounding and…'

'Even now?'

'What now?'

'Is the hounding still on?'

He rambled on, 'Even the morning when my mother was nowhere to be found and those security men surrounding our dunga.'

'Not found? What do you mean?'

'They accused us of letting go of a foreigner…first, being accused of keeping a foreigner till we'd gone all over trying to get hold of that nikahnama. She'd thrown away the original…blaming and cursing herself for marrying my father. He'd stuffed himself into another dunga, parked along the embankment at the other end.'

'Where? At which end?'

'Why talk of that useless stuff now?' Opening and closing his eyes with the bundle of those remains still clutched tight. 'This to be buried before…'

'Bury this right here, push this bundle into the ground.'
'Here?'
'Why not?'
'This place is…'
'The earth takes in just about anyone, anything!'
'But these remains are of a little child…barely a few months old, badly injured. Yesterday that man came asking for my father with this.'
'Some buyer of books?'
'From a bookseller he's been made into a butcher!'
'Some buyer of gosht then?"
'No! Father wasn't always a butcher. Hated slaughter. Hated fleshy chunks, hated meatballs!'
'Then?'
'Now forced to chop and cut…but that man who came looking for him wasn't any of the security creatures. He wasn't a foreigner, he was a Kashmiri—one of us. He had a worried look on his face. He sat on the grass and then walked around. Looked so nervous, couldn't walk properly. Then he handed Father these remains to be buried. Father was numb. Looked about dazed…kept sitting with the remains till the police van halted and pushed him into it for another round of chopping. So he handed them to me for burial.'
'Whose remains are these? Was it a relative or family?'
'Family? Everything's breaking apart!'
'Whose? This child?'
'Don't know. Just cut-up pieces beginning to curl up at the edges.'

'Stop! I can no longer take in all this!'

'Crawl on then. There are a few hours left for the sun to break.'

'Crawl more! How much more?' I asked incredulously.

'Away from this mess—before these creatures get to us. This is a dangerous zone, very dangerous. See that there.' He pointed to the tame waters of the springs running gently along the expanse that overlooked an outdated dak bungalow—a concrete-and-brick structure with makeshift floors. 'That's some kind of interrogation centre...those interrogations are on at every stretch,' he said, seeing me looking at the structure. 'Can't go back.'

'Nothing to go back to!'

'But you aren't from here...from those bhaiyya or Bihari places.' He stretched his lips to speak cuttingly, 'Seeking refuge here! Here! From where most are fleeing.'

'Refuge is beyond fleeing...it's a state of mind, from here to there.'

'You're saying this?'

'No, he'd said this...that man I'd lived with here.'

'Shhhh...not so loud,' he said, placing his mouth over mine, crushing my lips, rubbing his lips on mine, till the spectacles slid down. 'Don't speak at all.'

He made a complete turnaround. 'Want to go crawling right towards Muzaffarabad?'

'Muzaffaranagar!'

'No nagar or nagarpalikas...Muzaffarabad is where half of us Kashmiris live, but now can't talk about it. You can talk about what that big Partition did or undid, but we can't even think of our divided lands, of ourselves, of our missing folk! Our women going crying from jail to jail in search of their missing sons, husbands, fathers and grandfathers. Hundreds ruined around these Avantipoora ruins! The jails are clogged—the bloody prison holes are overflowing. Everyone's shoved into those holes, into those cells, worse than animal husbandry cells.'

Chapter 5

His grip was taut, then loosened. 'What was that? Lightning? Fire? No, no forest fires these!'

'There's a fire and…'

'Security creatures devouring everything in the open… there…out there.'

'They're cooking!'

'Feasting! Devouring bhairus, murgis, macchli… nothing left from that spread.'

'Saffron smells?'

'Third-class bloody bhaiyyas and zafraan! These unwashed creatures and delicacies!'

'Saffron…I smell saffron!'

'You people use our zafraan?'

'We'd use it in our bakery biscuits till those smells reminded us of the saffron brigade!'

'No saffron smells…saffron bulbs planted miles away, in

Pampar. Maybe saffron looted from our shops. Who knows? Everything's under their control. They live off our flesh here... I have not eaten a grain since noon. You?'

'Just something on that plane.'

'You came by air, not a bus? You can afford air tickets?' He stared at my face, my clothes and my bag. Like a lopsided sort of interrogation. He sat up, looking about agitatedly at the fires spreading with unabated fury. 'You landed here in some big plane!' Looking about, more than rattled. 'And they're devouring the forest...move on...move, let's get out of this stretch.'

'Together?'

'Dried chinars. Autumn...let's crawl behind those boulders and start moving towards that stream. Now just jump into it!'

'Snakes?'

'Kashmiri snakes are not like these creatures lurking around. Come on now, quick, move towards the waters.' He craned his neck to look ahead. 'There, there—where the shrubs are the thickest.'

'I can't. Can't crawl. My skin's tearing...how much further?'

'Miles beyond...towards...'

'Can't crawl anymore.'

Looking about helplessly, denting the monotony, he lashed his tongue nervously on the wide vacancy of my face. Lashed it a hundred times.

Was I committing adultery?

Re-lashing. My tongue kicking, licking, re-licking. Systematically. My fingers making sure that the somehow-stitched-back broken front tooth could contain the strain as his lips pressed on my mouth. He suddenly withdrew in some sort of disgust. 'Why're you fiddling with your hands?'

'Broken front tooth…this front one…it's stitched up.'

'My mother sits with three broken teeth…those side ones. Can barely bite, hardly eats now.'

He stared intently at my mouth. 'You're taking so long to even get your lips to mine!'

'Maybe I'm slow.'

'You're what?'

Taken aback by this sudden hormonal turbulence hitting me, I pulled him on me even as he tried to drift away an inch here or there. I clung on to him with the desperation of the desperate kind.

'Slide here. Don't know why I took on this madness,' he said as he placed his head next to mine. 'Let your mind wander away like the king of Hamadan transported himself from Central Iran to here, when Timur's wrath was unleashed on him. Let your mind wander, move away from…'

'I know what you mean. Without moving an inch from our dunga, he'd transported me all over the Valley…all over.'

'Who? Which man?'

'What do you mean, which one?'

'You're still on the lookout?'

'Crawling! For what? For him!'

'He's still in your head!'

'Yes, he's inside my head, all over me. He believed in making the mind wander from here and there, even towards the grave of Yousuf Aza and beyond...'

'You mean the grave of Yuz Asaph? You know about that grave?'

'He'd talk about graves and graveyards, describing them minutely.'

'You visit graveyards?'

'My father and brother lie buried in a qabristan.'

'Here?'

'Not here. In Bareilly. In my town. Kutcha graves. Now not to be found...the earth has consumed them.'

'Yuz Asaph's grave is 8-9 feet or more! That grave is so different!' He looked about as though looking for those bygones. 'Bodies lie buried, but their spirits move about freely. When I sit at these dargahs, I feel sukoon, otherwise I become restless. Do you understand? Do you know about Yuz Asaph's grave?'

'He told me that it belonged to one of Moses's descendants.'

'Have you read *The Fifth Gospel*?'

'No. What's that?'

'It's a book by Kashmiri historian Fida Hassnain, along with a Jew called Dahan Levi. Written on that big grave, it says that those three wise men who visited Bethlehem were Buddhists and that they'd found baby Bodhisattava. It also throws hints that Jesus visited Sind on the river Indus!'

'Many come to visit it?' I asked.

'Always one or two foreigners there between those weeds and the rubble...those creatures can't believe that such a long grave exists.'

'Goras?'

'Some speaking English, but don't know who's who these days.'

Seeing the hopelessness on my face, he quickly carried on, 'But do know that death does come. Graves and more graves getting unearthed. Unmarked graves along the Jhelum embankment and...'

'This...'

'What's this?' He suddenly stopped as he felt me pulling myself away from his grip to tear strips from the loose ends of my kurta and stuff them into my underwear.

He watched as I repeated the exercise. 'Stuff it... If they see me carting you around bleeding like this, they'll probably put murder charges on some wretched head!'

'On your head!'

'No. Someone else's. That's the way it works here...they will catch a passer-by!' he muttered.

'One of the outsiders moving about?'

'Don't know whether they're from the Indian intelligence or others. Days of captures and ruptures. Bloody mess! This bloody verse for your bloody flow— *Why from top to bottom, are you dressed in red!/What does it signify!/ Are these clothes perhaps stained /With the blood of someone wrongly slain!*'

'Your lines?'

'No, no. Not sure who's.'

'He would have known.'

'Who?'

'The man I lived with knew every little thing, every single line...without moving from his dunga he took me here and there, all over.'

'Till where?'

'All over...to Charar and Por. All through his talks. He'd tell me that those Sufis still yielded power, their roohs were still around.'

'Charar is many miles away from here! We've been there many times, even during the urs of Nund Rishi. We also went further up another mountain where lie the remains of the Iraqi Sufi Syed Ali... Sufis who'd come all the way from Iraq and Iran, never went back. They're buried in those graves, but their spirits move around... Even now if a man looks in the direction of Sufi Syed Ali's family graves at Por, he'll go blind.'

'Who told you this?'

'Father.'

'Your father? Rattling off those details while settling hides?'

'He's been giving commentaries. There's not one around to match him. These bloody security creatures have caught hold of him and forced him to cut and chop. Otherwise we'd be dead. Even after seeing so many deaths, he sits unmoving. Like the unmoving waters. Talking about these unmoving waters to those who hang around him. He says Muslims are obsessed with the flowing waters whereas non-Muslims prefer stagnant water. That's why the Hindu rajas created water tanks and the Musalmaans created the flowing waterfalls.'

'He knows all this?'

'Even that Bengali staying here carries too much knowledge of lakes, tanks, waterfalls, boats.'

'Which Bengali?'

'Which one? This one loafing around.'

'That bad one near that embankment and…'

'Who is good or bad? Are you good? The way you're crawling around like a wild animal in this wilderness?'

'But I'm…'

'Can't trust you or her. Last night she was heading into that dunga in control of that security inspector. All sorts of things happen in there!'

'Sex scandals?'

'Maybe other things…'

'But sex is a full-time job!'

'Not for people here like your cities! Your coming here all alone in this madness…even if I'm far away from Lal Chowk, I'm unsure of the next day. Of the danger of being thrown into an interrogation centre.'

'For what?'

'For chanting verse! For moving around from here to there…for anything! Stop this useless talk when there's a fear of being pulled apart, of being made to stand hunched like some bhairu or a murderer or whatever. The only thing these hands haven't done is to bang them on this head! I'm losing my head…these hands have begun to bother me, I'm going insane! There's nothing else in sight!'

'Nothing in sight? Where are all the roads? That road going to the mountain towards the springs, towards Zeashta Devi shrine and that Bhavan?'

'You've been there and back without getting ripped apart? Birds can't fly on that side of the sky. They'd be shot dead mid-flight! The security didn't drag you?' he sounded shocked.

'He closed his eyes, saying that Hazrat Bal was right in front of us. He asked me to imagine that lane which sold wicker stuff, describing the shops and the saffron-selling ones.' I craned my neck as though Hazrat Bal wasn't really beyond the reach of imagination.

'You know so much, being an outsider!'

'So many outsiders around!'

'Only some manage! That gora who's mad about cleansing the Dal seems to know the rest of them…knows them by their first names!'

'Where's he from? America or Australia?'

'Calls himself Vilayati Williams, so from Vilayat.'

'Vilayat? Musalmaans also name their sons Vilayat!'

'And still hacked by those goras. This Bengali doesn't go towards that Vilayati man, tries to ask us about houseboats and carvings on teak and what not…don't know whether she's from your Calcutta or Chittagong, but calls herself

South Asian.'

'But coming here all that way to this place…for what?'

'What's left of this place? It's breaking apart. There's already a partition between the KPs and us—what the British did earlier…now there are talks of dividing the state. Killings on. KPs moving into your India, but we're suspects everywhere—here or there. KPs marrying outside, but here, only fools drifting away. Only idiots marry…that Waheeda marrying Wahid's son but it wouldn't last a day.'

'Divorces rising?'

'Security creatures beat him right there!'

'What! Why?'

'Everybody knows.'

'Then?'

'Qaiser's with her…so many times…every day.'

'And these foreigners doing what?'

'Who knows what? Don't know why I'm telling you this. We'll probably be killed soon,' he whispered. 'This Qaiser's carrying information for the security. He was brought up by them. They slaughtered the rest and brought him up for this. He would have been dead long ago, his neck twisted. He now sits infected, vomiting stories of those high-ups. Spills out even names and surnames. He entered many of your Dilli women, and then caught the big infection from one when she'd spread herself for him after spreading out for others—men, women, cooks, crooks moving from bed to bed, not even sparing animals!'

'What rubbish!'

'You people go hand-in-hand with Amreekans...waiting for them to open base here. There are already many of them roaming about in disguise here. Qaiser says that Pahalgam is full of shaloms! Do you understand what it means? Jews, Israelis...they'll do what they've done in Palestine and much beyond. My father's been saying this for years.'

'Not arrested?'

'Life's hell for us!'

'But...'

'Arrests all over! Those schoolboys arrested for taking part in the burial procession of an Afghan! Why're you looking so dumbstruck? It's frightening! Till last year, Inayat Shah refused to marry his daughters outside Srinagar, but now he's packing them off. In another fit, he just got back both his sons from that boarding school, they'd been ragged and labelled kharkus! All this humiliation is not new for us. In fact, John Platts had described us Kashmiris as dancing women. Ongoing Western propaganda by those goras. And a new advisor is getting posted here. Some Musalmaan, but a politician they say; going for lal batti cars that screech and howl like owls or crazy foxes.' His monologue finally came to an end.

He nervously pushed his long strands back with his hands.

'I wanted to go to Lebanon, but no...the inspector's saying Khalil Gibran's days are over. Those philosophy days are over! Told me I'd mingle, or what he called, "intermingle" with the Hezbollahs.'

He continued, 'No, no, I had no intention of mingling or intermingling with anyone. I wanted to research Gibran's so-called love affair. He'd loved one woman and that too without sexual desire…he kept it going without any wants, all those twenty years, he'd controlled his sexual urges. They sabotaged my going…but before that, that inspector was trying to inspect my parts!'

'You read Gibran?' I was surprised.

'You sound like that bloody inspector. Anything wrong with that? Gibran's philosophy takes care of disturbances.'

'Can't save you from death though.'

'Yes, but neither does carrying ID cards which are being distributed, as Qaiser says, like free condoms. Our limbs are easy targets. That shopkeeper was shot dead at Lal Chowk, right in front of me. There's death all round. These political jokers don't seem to have heard of Shakespeare's line, "What's a town without people?" Deaths leave dents. More deaths, more crackdowns. Sadists give pain and humiliation, even in dreams.'

'What if somebody doesn't dream?'

'There's something here that makes you dream. Daydream about what you're looking for, that man and…'

'He'd speak to me for hours, his talks had kept me going.'

'You're leaving your home to hear him? Strange stories these…face the reality…pick up your spectacles and look through them.'

'You people never moved beyond this Valley?'

'Father did. But doesn't talk about it.'

'But your brother drives beyond it?'

'Only here. In Dilli, these bloody men had caught him for questioning. Threw his name into the police records and thrashed him.'

'What about you?'

He dragged my hand to place it on his penis. Somewhat erect, somewhat limp. It shrank a little as I moved my rather reluctant hand over it.

'Feel me…here,' he said again.

'You're cut up, stitched up there?'

'That's my circumcision mark.' He was instantly suspicious. 'You don't talk like a Muslim. Are you a Musalmaan or fooling around?'

'Stop it!'

'Outsiders moving around with Muslim names and surnames. One governor planted himself in some masjid, as a maulvi sahib, then hopped into a boat, fitted Urdu couplets in his speeches; another had…' he growled. 'See what your stupid talks have done! See! Broken tooth, circumcisions, cuts, marks! I'm turning limp! Aren't you a Muslim? Don't you know of our Musalmaan customs? Circumcision prevents infections. It can save lives, but no longer now. The kar sevaks at Babri Masjid marked them out—killing all those found circumcised. I don't know whether it's true or not, but even in some police stations in your India, they go by these marks.'

'What?'

'Heard it myself…Qaiser telling that Bengali.'

'So to remain alive should one be circumcised?'

'It depends on who's ruling and whom.'

'What if you had a son?'

He moved his head right and left, with a strange determination on the face, his large eyes opening and shutting tight. 'A child? No. No child for me!'

'You'd throw it out into these waters?'

'Those factories, grants and sanctions don't move beyond Jammu…these babus go after five women every night and another three during the day. They pick up innocents. My home is not far from that interrogation centre. We hear those deafening shrieks every day. It's worse than a slaughterhouse.'

'Your home?'

'A rented dunga, atop the Nageen. We're living like refugees.'

'Aren't refugees living in Jammu?'

'Those tents are worse than these hellholes I've heard Zafar describing. He's visiting Jammu, tucked that woman Sultana away somewhere there, but now says that even that's no longer safe. Thrown his son in Dilli. He's living there with a changed name, changed it to some KP name so that your police doesn't run after him.'

He paused. 'I don't ever imagine I'd change my name. Know too much about what happens. That minorities minister coming up with theories of chopping off names by a half or three quarters. Even if they pull out each one of my limbs, I will not sell myself. Even if they pull out all these nails, I would not stoop to the police. It's better to die than to live in these wretched times. That Buddhist married a non-Kashmiri and is openly out with her; that other fellow gives his outhouse to that third-class woman, but there are different rules for us. We are bribed to change names. Whilst we Kashmiris are surviving on weeds, these creatures host wazwaans, squeeze pashminas into their aunts' cunts!'

'Have you seen it happen?'

'Heard about it. Seen it. Read about it. Killed from each side. No, don't want my child to go crawling here. He'd stand hunched, stammering...be picked up. On the charge of having an Afghan parent or grandparent. I see a hopeless look on my mother's face, calling out to me in the middle of the night, muttering that she's moving herself from here. Don't know what she has in her mind... She wants to go back. Sits muttering names of some mohallas and gullees.'

'Does she still have relatives in Afghanistan?'

'Nobody.'

'Then?'

'What?'

'There has to be someone...anyone?'

'Must you ask so many questions? You will not last long here. Why are you not going back?'

'Go back, go back! Where do I go back to? After crawling this far?'

He rolled his eyes. 'Not sure whether we'll ever be able

to move out of here.'

'Take me out of here. Take me back…back to my dunga.'

'That Bengali takes one backwards. Have been telling Qaiser to stay far away from this woman creaking around the wooden floors.'

'Breaking?'

'Creaking. When that security creature makes his way in, it creaks when…'

'Which creature? Can he help me?'

'Are you mad? He'd first suck out your broken tooth and then throw your remains in some gutter!' he snarled.

'I want to get out of here.'

'I'm not sure I can help you do that. Not sure of anything anymore. These remains with me, nothing. Now slide and move this bag. What's inside it?'

'Clothes and chits!'

'ID proof?'

'No, no. He'd given me two chits carrying my name and…'

'That man you lived with gave you your name? What the hell are you mumbling about?'

'He gave me an additional name, just in case…'

'Just in case you forget your own name!'

'He threw these chits into my hands just days before I was thrown into that van.'

'What!'

'Just two names scribbled on two chits…bits of paper.'

'Were they not pulled out during those searches?'

'Had tucked them here, into me…right under this…'

'Your hands are trembling…there's blood trickling from these fingers.'

I startled him with my hands as they travelled from my head towards his. Pulling him closer, I met his gaze. Hitting out at my double crossing—seeking refuge in his body whilst on the lookout for another man.

I slapped my hands on my forehead. For this strange contradiction, for this urge for him that was sweeping through me.

Chapter 6

Compelling conversions continue at an amazing pace. Stubbornly unmoving. Somewhat settled, to be repeatedly re-settled in the midst of a well-creased session with rebels quite simply having their way.

Fingers moving about. No, not to check on that once-upon-a-time fallen tooth. This time along his falling strands. Moving on his face before running on his stomach, then along the sides of his face. Licking his face as though a dairy whitener had accidentally fallen over it. Onwards, to his hips, towards that somewhat-shrunk penis.

Till, with a wild look in his eyes, he finally reacted. Balls whirlpooling along with the strain of the stream. Offloading that overburdened posture. Set to deliver. Unsure, but stealthily stretching his hands in slow motion. Mumbling. In just a couple of hours, they'd become addicted to moving along my form. Like an overburdened sex enthusiast, opening and closing the legs at regular intervals. Like an unmanned railway phatak at the outer municipal limits of a mufassil township. Shutting and opening for the overspeeding Punjab Mail or for the lethargically slow Bareilly Express.

He was dishevelled and distraught, not quite stagnant and static, though obviously stranded in the midst of a stillness of sorts. As his eyes closed and opened anxiously, his mouth came near mine and his lips explored my face.

Suddenly, he did a complete turnaround. 'Forwards or backwards? Run somewhere. But where? Towards Pampar? Pampar—where those bulbs sprout and the saffron smell spreads, where lies Lalla Arifa. No, no it's not her, it's Habba who gets me restless.' His lips move restlessly, muttering, *'Love has consumed me from within/ He has cast me into a hot oven/ And is burning me to cinder/ Love has melted me like the snow/ He has fretted me like the hill stream/ And has made me restless like the rills…'*

'Where did you learn these?'

He ignored me.

'There's a head, a body…something's in that stream.'

'What is it?'

'Some sort of floating greenish mass out there.'

He threw me a side glance. 'More around Dal, vegetables growing on these. I know my land. Every inch of it…all about it. Lawrence writes about the parallel between the Chinampas of Old Mexico and our floating gardens in that lake.'

'Can't it be uprooted?'

'The uprooted cannot adjust.'

'Set afloat elsewhere? So many fleeing and resettling in Jammu.'

'Pull out a tree, try replanting it. It just droops—it's difficult striking roots!'

'There's another, but it's sinking.'

'Can't you throw yourself in it—float or swim?'

'Can you?'

'Of course I can. I'm a Kashmiri. It is my birthright to float in a stream or nullah. But we must throw ourselves in or get killed by these creatures. No other way out to transport yourself from here to there.'

'From here to where?'

'Let the mind float or move backwards. Qaiser says this Bengali takes you back.'

'Moving backwards? Where?'

'To where you were conceived.'

'Even those uprooted ones?'

'Don't know, but Qaiser says she takes you right back. He says that everything in life depends on where one has been conceived. She asked him about politicians, the police. She told him that the children conceived during curfews have unhappiness in their marrow.' He pushed back the hair falling on his face and partially on mine. 'She tells all sorts of things. If your mind revolts, then don't part your legs. Semen drops, not nasal drops, are released into clogged openings. She tells him this! Tells him that weaklings get release like this.'

'Like you're doing right now?'

'You talk shamelessly. Not like a Musalmaan woman.'

'What about you?'

'I shouldn't. I shouldn't be shoving myself into you. No, no not in these times…when I can hear the prisoners scream.'

'Then why're you doing it?'

'Qaiser says men can't keep sperm jailed!'

'Uff!'

'That's the way he talks, not me!'

'He says all this?'

'Moves about like a stray dog moves at night!'

'At night? Why?'

'Many line up at the Bengali's place at night. Qaiser says daytime is risky.'

'Is he married?'

'He's a stray animal. Trained by this bloody security to dig out marrow. They've stuffed his head since he was a child. They've finished him off—eaten into his skull. My brother says they systematically ruined him, trained him to dig into flesh, to catch hold of dead intestines, to dig into anything to get information.'

'Where was he conceived?'

'No idea.'

'What about you? Were you conceived here?'

'What?'

'You…er, where were you conceived?'

'How can you even ask?'

'Didn't your father ever talk of this?'

'My father! Talk of this?'

'Maybe you were conceived in the mind…in your father's head!'

'Then trickled down.'

'Down but not out.'

'Dangerous!'

'Dangerous? Conceiving is dangerous?'

'Depends…but first conceived in the head, then goes trickling down…'

'Maybe.'

'I was conceived here but my mother was not conceived here.'

'What're you mumbling?'

'My mother's not from here, so not conceived here.'

'Your mother told you this?'

'Who else? She was conceived in the Ali Zai mohalla of a small town where fleeing Afghans had settled in Uttar Pradesh. But she herself had to flee from there.'

'What? All this your mother told you?'

'Yes! She'd tell my brother and me, nobody else was there; Father had moved far away…lived away.'

'Your father's people are here?'

'Dead and gone. Grandfather's big house on the way to the airport near a school was set in flames. They'd searched our home, thrown out my father's books—he had thousands and thousands of rare books in his library, and newspapers piled up there—I remember how they destroyed everything. They burnt it all down...as though each little book was a suspect of some kind. They ruined us...we had to flee towards Charar and beyond, hiding here and there. Later my father started living in some dunga till this summer, when that too was destroyed by that security inspector hell-bent on ruining him.'

'Your mother's not around?'

'Don't you listen? Been telling you that she has that half-Afghan tag pinned on her. She's now been thrown out of that ward to God knows where! Maybe into those prison hellholes where foreign suspects are dumped.'

He raised his head for a fraction of a second, then almost as an afterthought placed it back on my breasts. The cleavage provided sufficient hiding ground. Then, almost as suddenly, he ducked. Seeking refuge. Even as the breasts lay sagging, hopelessly drooping, giving up the struggle to play the diverse roles.

He touched my face on either side and brought his face next to mine, staring intensely. Then withdrawing. Then raising his head and pulling up the tainted pyjamas, before pulling himself away.

His expressions kept changing. Wondering and wandering. Whether his father's sperms had trickled down inside a stranded form in the midst of a cushioned floor or atop a rectangular bed made of walnut wood. Or was it a quick putting together of plain planks of the weeping willow? No, that would be too simple. And a carved walnut-wood structure far beyond reach. Was he conceived during a release session or in the midst of some emotional outburst that his parents seemed quite capable of? In between those breaks from diversions, towards the supposed unthinkable terrain—could his father have touched and re-touched several other women? His mother looked severely under-touched. She often said there seemed little reason for her to live on. How often she'd sit and stare as though strangely stranded in some strange settings! Rather obviously mismatched were the two, yet they didn't part ways. There were times when he was tempted to ask his mother how she'd ended up with his father, yet couldn't. Those strains of hurt lurking around her eyes seemed too absolute to be hurt once again by being asked.

He distracted himself, creating dents in those thoughts as his fingers moved about, then stopped, inside me. He frowned and suddenly stopped, as though angry with himself for these ongoing intrusions. He tried to withdraw. Till my tongue took charge. Thrusting, lashing his teeth. Re-lashing his front teeth, one slightly edged over the other, clasping each other with an unspoken want, relaying a bonding. Before the two sets of teeth could clash, emitting warlike sounds. Apprehensions riding and overriding, of my tooth getting dislodged and getting lodged in his mouth. Right into one of his long-winding intestines.

His fingers moved along my stomach, intensely touching the terrain, making sure the ovaries and the uterus were still tucked in, whilst offloading a strange sort of commentary.

Hadn't he heard that quack who'd quacked all the way from Jammu, sitting under one of those aging chinars quite firmly rooted along the outer road? Quacking all the way about the new forms of conversions. Those stuck or semi-stuck, selling off vital organs, plucking them off from those hideouts in the very anatomy.

He clutched himself, crying out in a low tone about 'that MLA whatever that rascal's name, ordering the SHO to pluck out ovaries and healthy testicles…he was screaming, he didn't want drooping or bloated testicles but those of teenagers. The next morning five boys went missing from our area.'

'Disappeared?'

'Ready to part with their organs!'

'For how much?'

'Not for money. For releases.' He shook his head hopelessly. 'For the release of their fathers, grandfathers and brothers who'd gone missing.' He cried as if he were joining the queue of those readying themselves for seasonal plucking. Flinging words about. Flitting from one sequence to another, from digging gaping graves in the midst of a barrenness of sorts to the wooden-planked dungas with Kashmiri motifs holding ground amidst a nothingness of sorts.

His lips quivered next to my cold ear. 'My father was not always a butcher! He was turned into one by these security men. Now he can even pull out rabbits from their burrows and hack them!'

'Rabbiting?'

He nibbled my stomach with his front teeth. Digging deeper. He stretched my legs, opening them wide. Making up for the stretch of months when my legs parted and re-parted with nothingness in between, even as a way of gesture or protocol or formality.

He shook his head. As if trying to drill some sense into it. He quickly pulled my legs together. 'Nothing's to be born, nothing's to be conceived here.'

'You were conceived...er, where?'

'And you?'

'Why're you going on and on about the same stupid thing?'

'That woman says conceiving time is crucial for times to come...takes you right back. Says they're the ones who build the houseboats. Says Akbar had got Bengali craftsmen to build them...Akbar the blue-blooded Mughal emperor who had turned red by the time he got to formulating the new religious order, Din-i- Ilahi.'

'Why're you repeating all this historical stuff?'

'She says she's craving for roots, for those who built wooden getaways. She's mad about anchorage.'

'I can't understand all this!'

'Says that hides can't hide forever if unhappiness lies tucked in the marrow.'

'What does that mean?'

'Can't be described...this is what she chants.'

'Chanting such rubbish. And you're all believing her!'

He pushed his face below. And then quite suddenly asked, 'You were conceived in your Bareilly?'

I looked away, upset and angry for being born.

Lying listless in Shukoh's arms, I wondered forlornly where I could have been conceived.

Somewhere in the mango grove? No, the two wouldn't have allowed themselves to touch each other out there under clusters of trees and more trees, with their ever-widening branches spreading out. No, no, not whilst they were crawling about. But why should they have been crawling? Little need for that as they lived in better times, moved about freely from here to there…everywhere…except to Pakistan. There seemed to be some sort of apprehension amidst suspicion and more of those officially called free flows. My father refused to go to the LOC even when he got the news of his brothers dying in Lahore. 'No!' he'd said, amidst a migraine tearing through his head and throwing up. 'These government creatures here would grab these orchards like those chief minister's men barged into Askari Ahmad's haveli, trumpeting that it was state-owned… that deputy collector has anyway been asking whether we're crossing over to what he calls the new country for the Musalmaans!'

Maybe I was conceived during one of my father's outbursts on the Partition—which had become weaker and weaker as he started falling into depression, before getting sucked into the forgetfulness of his mind. Just he and those orchards, emotions getting tighter and tighter till almost choked lay those memory cells. With that, my mother had become subdued on my marriage front, though quite often she'd rant about there being a time, a suitable time, for a woman to have children. Little must she have imagined even in her wildest nightmares that I would conceive in the midst of this chaos.

Chapter 7

It was like the trickles from a leaking inkpot. Those bloody stains spreading around, along with those half-sentences Shukoh threw out. 'This? What's all this?'

'This bloody flow month after month!'

'What?'

'Not happening to your mother?'

'What about her?'

'Your mother doesn't have these menstrual flows?'

'Why're you dragging my mother into this rubbish?'

'Women are the same everywhere.'

'No. Our women, our history...'

'History! Quoting history on my dying head!'

'Our women...our women mystics...'

'Women are the same all over, they live in pain, suffer their husbands and what not!'

'Our Kashmiri mystics, Habba Khatoon, Lalla Arifa,

were saddled with bad husbands. Lalla went about chanting that she'd not seen a single man till she spotted Shah-e-Hamadan here.'

'Taking refuge in your long-winding history, huh?'

'You're taking refuge here too. Our women drowned their sorrows in verse. Lalla hummed, *Think not on the things that are without/ Fix upon thy inner self thy thought/ So shall thou be freed from let or doubt/ Precepts these that my Preceptor taught./Dance then Lalla, clothed but by the air/ Sing then Lalla, clad but in the sky. Air and sky: what garment is more fair?/Cloth said Custom. Doth be that sanctity?*'

'How do you know these lines?'

'I've read all possible books… Have you read the *Kashir* volumes?'

'Read those two *Kashir* volumes in that dunga. He used to keep them high up on that shelf. Those pages that have everything about you Kashmiris, but not a single thing about your sex lives!'

'Sex?'

'Yes, sex.'

'Why beat your chest?'

'You're the one who said that sperms can't linger…they need to be released!'

'Qaiser's words, not mine!' His nostrils flared. 'I can smell something…the Bengali's dunga carries these smells.'

'Throwing her bloody-soaked stuff all around as if it's her Bay of Bengal. What else?' I asked sarcastically.

'You throwing your bloody leaks on me! Let me

survive…these smells are nauseating!'

'I could never have imagined that I'd be crawling around this way… I don't want to be thrown back, don't want to flee… I want to survive till I find my man, my child.'

'The Kashmiris are the actual survivors. Surviving to write. What poets this place has produced—Ghani's verses haunt… *He who clings to his birthplace will know no freedom from trouble; while the rose clings to her stem, thorn-pricks are close to her flesh.* He knew that a day would come when hundreds would flee…it was like a forewarning.' He looked about strangely. 'Forewarning, yet people land!'

'Those Sufis have been running from their land…they never ever went back to the countries they fled from.'

'Today's Afghans are fleeing from those Amreekans… to be hounded and rounded up. Holding them by their hair, dashing their heads around!' His stale breath hit me as he craned his neck, changing gear, from the first straight to the third. 'These Amreekans' research centre's big office on Boulevard…that office with hundreds working on Yuz Asaph! All those books on him were okay, but landing their bloody agents here to write and what not!'

'Have you read those books also?'

'Yes, I've seen better days. My father, grandfather and even his father were into books.'

'Then?'

'What then? Things change. Why're you here? You were born there in your Bareilly or whatever the name of that town is, but now crawling here in these tatters!' Looking at me rather too intently, he continued, 'Your Bareilly people won't recognize you! Who knows what's to happen? Those Sufis born in Central Asia lie dead thousands of miles away. Did their mothers know that this would happen? Mothers running wildly for the release of their sons. Going hysterical, running about, killed by the dozen, yet that institute to protect human rights keeps its gates shut. Running on sarkari dole…blank cheques handed out for holding seminars on our personal law!'

He slowed down a bit, but not before slow screaming into my ear, holding on to me in a strangely aggressive way, 'We've gone through hell! Down these years, these centuries.'

'Hell is what we are going through right now!' I said indignantly.

'This crawling is nothing if you read about what we went through in those years. The Sikhs, Afghans and Dogras treated us Kashmiris like animals. They thought no more of cutting off Kashmiris' heads than plucking flowers. Throwing the dead around like crumbs.'

'Okay, stop now, I cannot listen to this anymore. I'm dying here. Cannot crawl anymore, these hands, these legs, this…'

'This is nothing if you read what that traveller Moorcroft writes of Sikhs treating us Kashmiris like cattle. G.T. Vigne also writes of the tyrannical suppression of the Chaks, and that Frenchman Jacquemont describes tortures and…'

'Why don't you write about this crawling?'

'I will, if left alive! These bruises…'

Looking at his own hands, throwing them about wildly as though keeping them alive just about somehow. 'So much to write about the Kashmiri language, about the very name of this place…I know a lot—all facts. Not twisting them to make communal tales like these politicians are doing. The way your Indian historians go after Aurangzeb…hell, there's a minister in your Dilli who's named his dog Aurangzeb!'

'But Aurangzeb…'

'Was what? Everything's been twisted. Who can't twist? I can twist things…create a communal controversy about any damn thing.'

'Stop dumping all this on my head.'

'When you're crawling on my land, then you have to listen to all this…these are facts about my Valley.'

'Just don't go on and on. I know all this!'

'Taught in your schools and colleges?'

'No. He told me.'

'Did he also tell you that just one whisper of Afghans, Banglas, Pakistanis can get you arrested double quick?'

'So blatant?'

'Yes, they stand out! Standing out as black and white, as Qaiser says, like one's sexual preferences.'

'Why talk all this rubbish?'

'Says it's a side business, says latest is cards complete with sexuality status—trisexual, bisexual, all lies stuffed into it…says some new madness, these sexual preferences.'

'Where's this Qaiser?'

'Roams around…can't revolt or run away.'

'Is he dangerous?'

'Dangerous? Everyone's dangerous! Everyone's doing dangerous things. Even this. Crawling. Even this biting is…' He looked at me strangely and shoved his fingers inside my mouth, stretching it wide open. 'Show me…this tooth, this broken tooth of yours. Is it artificial or your own?'

'My own. Stitched back. This one…the right one. Don't touch it.'

'You've been biting like a wild animal!' His fingers hopped gently from one tooth to the next, checking and cross-checking. 'They say one should massage the gums with the fingers and not with a brush. Anyway…my dentist sahib also gone. He was a good man, a good dentist but…'

'To Jammu?'

'To some bloody jail, for settling a mujahidin's broken teeth.'

'A militant?'

'Why're you getting into useless arguments? They're the same for us, call them by any name.' His fingers stopped moving. 'Call these teeth daant or teeth or whatever—will make very little difference.'

His focus shifted temporarily as he continued rubbing his fingers across them, gently touching and re-touching my teeth with his fingers. All the while talking about his own teeth. 'Two wisdom-carrying teeth revolted till they were pulled out. Once and for all. Dentist sahib knocked off two of the side ones, calling us for those settling and resettling sessions. But all that was years ago. Now not a rupee left for any of these teeth-settling sessions.'

'You went about settling your teeth!'

'No, no, my father was obsessed with teeth, his and ours…not my mother's…he didn't even bother when she'd cry out in pain.'

'Mine broke while I was climbing a mango tree in our orchard. I hit my face on the branch and this front one broke.'

'Climbing trees?'

'Now none of those, trees, orchards, our home, belong to us anymore.'

'You didn't fight?'

'I was petrified that they'd kill me in some encounter.'

'Encounters reaching your Bareilly? Haven't heard of this. Never read this.' He threw up his hands. 'But not read a thing for many weeks now—now for me it's just digging, burying the dead.'

He picked a small berry from one of the drooping branches and threw it into my hand, gesturing that I use my side teeth.

'Do you have a knife? This tooth, and…'

He looked at me wide-eyed. 'Don't get those new things…they're no good.'

'You know about implants?'

'Of course I do. But those implants haven't reached here as yet, from Vilayat or that cowboy belt.' He looked at the berry with wild intensity. 'I'll break it and then…'

'Do you have a knife on you?'

'A knife's enough to get me arrested! There are special laws for us Kashmiris.'

'You know about laws?'

'Of course I do. I went to Burn Hall School.'

'You went to Burn Hall? Then?'

'Then nothing. So many others also not paying their fees like me.'

'But are you a postgraduate or…?'

'Graduation, post-graduation done privately, studied sitting at home, amidst those books. What else?' He plucked a few more berries and threw them towards my face.

'You know, this Bengali woman uses some sort of stick in the mouth.'

'For what?'

'For cleaning that rot in her mouth…keeps walking here and there, spitting in front of her dunga with that stupid board dangling, "Rabbits Do It All The Time."'

'A board and you noticed it?'

'Noticed it? Seen it! Read it too!'

'I want to see it. Take me there.'

'It's miles away.'

'Is it already midnight?'

'That's when the day begins for Qaiser.'

※

He looked at his wristwatch, its hands dangling free. As

freely as his own hands. Stretching. To see the changing expressions on mine. He placed his mouth next to mine with his lips moving on it.

All too suddenly, he became a different person. 'Run from this mess. But where to? Security forces all around! Unhappiness clinging…spreading around.'

'You're carrying these smelly remains…clinging to them as though they were conceived here!'

'There's no set place for conceiving. Can happen anywhere—just like you leaking everywhere! You were conceived where?'

'Didn't I tell you?'

'Just cross-checking!'

'Conceived in the head! You?'

'Maybe conceived amidst turbulence.'

'But then it was peaceful.'

'Could've been the turbulence hitting the head.'

'Bringing in heads and tails!'

'You tell me—where the hell were you conceived?'

'Me?'

'Yes, you! I've been talking endlessly.'

'Certainly in my hometown, in my home, my father hated shifting…would rarely move out.'

'Not even towards the mountains?'

'No, never. Those mountain ranges were miles away…but yes, sometimes we travelled to Nainital in my grandfather's Dodge.'

'Dodging? Car dodging its way.' A wry smile spread

on his lean face…perhaps for the first time his face looked somewhat calm.

'No one went dodging.'

'Your father didn't drive?'

'Yes, he did,' I replied. 'First an old Baby Hindustan, then a new Fiat. Drove so very cautiously, but see, nothing could prevent our ruin…if he'd been alive today and seen me crawling like this, he'd die a thousand deaths. He never wanted anything to come in the way of our happiness but now…'

'Mountains, trees, forests, nothing stands in the way. Now all shrivelled and uprooted lie these trees, contractors fixing up contracts with these sarkari men!'

'No arrests?'

'Arrests of these contractors? No way.'

'No stopping them?'

'Who can stop them? Who can stop destructions and demolitions! That Babri Masjid near your town? The way they pulled it down.'

'That masjid was far away from Bareilly but we were attacked just after that. Our home was destroyed. They were searching for…'

'For?'

'No gold biscuits! Only stale atta cookies. They pulled down the bakery, the doors and windows. They killed and smashed heads!'

'Nothing left here anymore. Everything's gone. I've stopped writing too. The IB's getting translators to read between the lines. Those bloody Bihari cops thrashed that boy right there.'

'Rumours!'

'I knew you'd say this!'

'Next you'll repeat being beaten on your...'

'Not just here, but happening in your bhaiyya towns as well. That boy Arif was detained because he wouldn't let that bloody inspector go shoving himself into him! No other reason. He was arrested overnight. Until July, the poor boy was running around in your Dilli for college admissions and now sits imprisoned. Had to go to the police station for registration and it happened there. They told him to be quiet and not cry out otherwise he'll be slapped with terror charges! No wonder everyone's turning anti-establishment. What else to do with this zulm heaped on us? More and more crackdown specialists flown here to terrorize us.'

'More crackdowns?'

'Cracking skulls...most don't survive. Ruhela Rauf's son is missing. She's peeping into jails. Roohi involved with more than one minister, but can't trace her own sister's son.'

'These women are telling you all this?'

'Qaiser told me this. All those seminars all over the world about Kashmir taking place, discussing us and our barbaadi, but look at what's going on here? Security-wallahs sprawled in our gardens, lakes and meadows. Not even sparing schools, hospitals and homes. Right up to Maqdoom sahib's dargah...along the downtown lanes gazing at those chandeliers at Dastgeer sahib's dargah.

They're even stuffing themselves into our boats!'

'Doing what?'

'That inspector destroyed my father's books, his boat and everything else...forcing my father to cut and chop bakras and bhairus, running blades on their throats with a running commentary. They'd dragged him out. And he had to go otherwise he'd have been shot dead. Then they'd say, "See, we have killed another terrorist and get a padak or a sadak renamed!" He looked at me agitatedly. 'And here you land! Why here? What do you want?'

'I'm thirsty. This water, this stream...'

'Shallow waters strewn with boulders.'

'Fruit on the trees?'

'Yes, loaded. But who'll climb? Don't want to break my bones...got to somehow get back.'

'They'll be waiting for you?'

'Who?'

'Your brother the driver, and father...will they wait till you return after burying this bundle?'

'Don't call it a bundle! This is a child. My father sat with it for minutes, looked as though he'd burst out crying...not sure whose baby this is.'

'Ask the man who got it along. Maybe it's his child.'

'Didn't seem like it was his...don't know why my father kept kissing it so much—just like he would kiss our foreheads when we were little boys. He insisted I bury it properly, kept saying—bury this baby as though you are burying your brother.'

'How old is your father?'
'Why're you asking me all this?'
'Why not?'
'My father's old…more than sixty.'
'And still running away from home?'
'You tell me! You're running away from your own home too. Tell me!'
'Tell you what? What's left to say? I have told you all those details. Everything lies tucked here in this head, unmoving…even right now I can recall those chalk marks on the gates of my father's home and…'
'Your father's home or grave?'
'My father's grave is in the same town as his home.'
'You remember your home?'
'Haan. Even now it stands out.' The intrusions creeping in. Hitting me. Chalk marks. That nameplate, the aftermath. Restlessness building up and charging me up. I sit up startled from a stretched-out period of hibernation. Impatient to make up for those lost years. Those voices still echoing from various quarters. Countering, choking, suffocating. Superimposing additional tactics. The smudged chalk marks on the porch giving way to the fury of the mob gathered about ferociously, and then no longer so. Crumbling. Like that mosque succumbing to the fury of the saffron brigade.

Chapter 8

I held on to Shukoh...jolted from my period of hibernation, impatient to make up for those lost years. All I needed was a man who could hiss those words every woman yearns to hear. Never mind even if they're wrapped in a façade of long-winding sentences, high-sounding verse and even higher-sounding emotions.

'Who's left in your home now? Someone or no one?'

'What's wrong with your stupid head? Haven't I been telling you repeatedly—no one! No one. No one. No one there!'

'Here?'

'Searching for him. That man in that dunga.'

'Was the man a Kashmiri?'

'What else? I've been saying so all these hours!' I sat up to look at his fading form with fading expressions on his face.

'Where is he now?'

'Do you want me to die repeating this? I cannot keep on telling you the same old details. Didn't you listen to me earlier?'

'All seems to be slipping past...I can't understand much. Where is that man now?'

'He stood hunched as my child was pulled away from me. I was thrown into that police van and I never saw him again.'

'You're still on the lookout for that man...even now? Even after being with me all these hours?'

'Why do you think I'm crawling? Why? My knees are cracking and my hands are bleeding.'

'That man...what does he do?'

'Nothing much. He took me all over without moving, just talking.'

'I don't understand.'

'What's there to understand? I'm telling you whatever there is to say...he didn't do much except...'

'What?'

'Talk. Spoke for hours.'

'And you?'

'I listened. And now I've come back after all these months. They pulled me away...threw me into a van. They pulled down this shalwar, chucked some powder on me just like they were flinging grain to flock of pigeons. Then, patting the sides of these legs, my legs, they pulled out my child...my child!'

'Your child?'

'Yes, my child…yes, mine.'

'His?'

'His and mine.'

'Where's the child now?'

'I don't know. Somewhere. May be anywhere. Take me to those dungas along that embankment…maybe he's still there…still there looking after our child. Born on that wooden floor.'

'Such things happened here? You were living with that man here? Out there in the public!'

'Rarely moved out of that dunga.'

'Your child was born inside a dunga?' he repeated, not quite getting over it.

Pulling those tresses hanging rather helplessly around my face. Akin to state-run lullabies, my words tumbled out, 'I had nothing with me, just two chits…that's all to me. When they threw me into the van, they patted these breasts and even there…hiding nothing, just those two chits, which are still with me. Nothing to do with anyone. He'd given them to me—he had nothing else to give.'

'Where did you keep them?'

'With me…tucked them right into me. Well inside my flesh.'

'Into you? Show me.'

'You're not a cop for me to show them to you!'

'Then go crawling alone…get out of here,' he said angrily.

'But there are…those animals there.'

'Those seem like goats huddled to be slaughtered. Those security creatures must be feasting at the other end. Come on. Let's keep going. There's no other way, there's no one to help. You and your destiny!'

He didn't give up his hold on my shoulders. Hell-bent on trying to figure out my status or trying to fit himself into any of the familiar slots, he was looking straight into my eyes, camouflaging his sentiments, till his well-set eyes started growing in diameter and dimension, as if they had laboured out of the pelvic structure of a frenzied one. Not sure of the bygones and more than unsure of the incoming ones. Distant and dismal.

He raised his head and looked down, having second thoughts, making sure his limbs were still in contact with his form, touching and touching his arms. Then mine. Pushing out more words this time, 'Go crawling…nobody ever went back…none of those who'd come here for refuge ever went back to the way they'd lived earlier.'

He gazed intently at the hollowness around the shrubbery that camouflaged our forms.

'Keep crawling. Search for that child. Children in government orphanages are readied as informers to carry information from here to there.' His voice sounded urgent.

'Like your Qaiser?'

'Not the only one. There are hundreds more…'

'Which orphanage?'

'Not one, many. Keep crawling, or just sit deadened like my mother. Stuffed in those wards, right into their cells, she's shrieking for Afghani yakhni, salan, mohallas. She doesn't understand. You wouldn't understand, run…tell no one you've been with a Kashmiri, otherwise you'll be shoved into their interrogation cells.'

'Run from here to where? The fires are raging…that stream, those men, those animals. Where do I go?'

'Miles to go…you're bleeding from every quarter. My father said weights were no longer measured by those outdated ways. They were sabotaged by the British. He believed that those goras ruined us…the British governor general's role in that Afghan invasion and…'

'What's the point muttering about ruins when we ourselves are ruined?' I looked around at the hopelessness and slurred, 'Carry me to Por or Charar.'

'Those caretakers wouldn't let you in.'

'Towards Sopore's apple orchards,' I murmured.

'There's heavy security everywhere. It's seeped into every little inch.' He quickly tore his shirt at the loose ends and stuffed the shreds into my vagina. 'Stop this flow. If they see me carting you around, they'll twist this neck!'

I flung my arms around him, wrapping him with those traces of might still in my possession. His shirt was nowhere to be seen. A somewhat torn vest to counter the breeze. I held on to him with a frightening intensity. My lips moved about on his face, his mouth, the two inter-clasped front teeth, those cheekbones, ear lobes, neck…

He closed his eyes, and then opened them. No, not that they were looking at me accusingly. He mumbled that he'd buried too many to fear lying in the folds of the earth. He looked up at the sky changing into diluted hues. A wry smile stretched across his face as he remembered his mother's obsession with black and white; and his father's inevitable intervention of toning the two extremist shades, as he'd call them, with varying dilutions. Though those variations and submissions could never quite be bailed out, they were unrelenting in what they hounded. On some pretext or the other, the Afghan connection being the predominant one.

'Can't go on anymore…can't.'

'What're you saying?'

'The bones are sticking out, my skin is ruptured. Here, carry these remains. I cannot move any further.'

'Where do I go?'

'Anywhere. The night's passing by. Keep crawling and moving before they spot you…'

He stopped. Half-whispering, half-crying, murmuring, he could visualize himself being flung into one of those hellholes, with holes being drilled into his skull. Certain of death or a near-death situation; arrested under any one of the acts flourishing in the state.

'Shhhh…sit…sit still.'

'Show me the chits.'

'There's nothing on them…just a name scribbled on each.'

'Whose?'

'Mine.'

'Two names—to fool someone or what?'

'Meer gave them to me for any of those emergencies. Said to use my Muslim name in this Valley and change it to the Hindu name beyond it. Meer also said that at every check post they'd ask for my name, that's why…that's why he gave me those two chits long before I was dragged out by those…'

'Two names?'

'Yes. One my own name—Husna Hakeem—and the other, Deepti Kaul. He knew what's happening here. He was far ahead, could see much beyond.'

He looked at me strangely. 'What did he do…that man?'

'Tasted my saliva, lashed his tongue and…'

'Didn't he work anywhere? How did he feed you? How?'

'Those potatoes or…'

'Didn't he have to pay for that boat? Didn't he feed you anything other than those potatoes? Where did he get that damn money from?'

'It was his own boat. His sons looked after his wife and…'

'You met them…his wife and sons?'

'No…he kept them away, never met them. They lived on the Nageen side.'

'Nobody bothered you, nobody asked you anything? You were living with a man. These things don't happen here. It's impossible!'

'Take me to that embankment side. I will show you our dunga. Let us crawl forward or backward, whichever way, but out of here.'

'You won't find your man or child in this mess, you'll die here. You will die like us all—just the way my mother and father are dying.'

'Can your father help? Can't he find him?'

'He himself is in their hold…slitting throats for them. His own neck is on the line. Mention Afghan weaves and he pales.' He looks around, perhaps for those last-minute distractions. 'The police are hounding us, making us lose our heads. All he does is chop and cut.'

'Meer hated fleshy chunks. Just kept talking, saying no one knows who's doing what here!'

'He said this?'

'Who else? He trusted no one here…moved away, stuffed himself into that dunga.'

'What is his full name?'

'His name?'

'Yes, his name…the man you're searching for. What before or after Meer?'

'Meer…only Meer.'

He looked shocked. Then, trying to assemble or re-assemble his posture. 'Meer? That is every second person's name here. Even my father's name is Meer!'

'Yes, he did say that it was a very common name. He jokingly called himself Meer Taqi Meer...the long dead poet! He always laughed, saying that the dead don't die, so he has to be alive!'

'What? Repeat that! He called himself Meer Taqi Meer? My father also called himself that but...' Then, as if to dilute the shock, 'many add that Taqi bit.'

'But where's your father? Could he trace my Meer?'

'My father? He has no emotions. But I saw him looking somewhat okay only when he clasped this dead child. He'd kept kissing it, just as he used to kiss us. Maybe he's the same man...your Meer.'

'Same man? My Meer? But...'

He looked at me for a while and then clasped me tight. 'Keep crawling and don't mention any Afghan or Kashmiri connections ever. They'd drag you away. Don't utter your Musalmaan connection. Give some Buddhist name and you'd be spared being transported to those mountains up there!'

His eyes moved about, drifting into an oblivion of sorts, not keeping pace with the wild look in mine. I tried to sit up, faintly trying to repeat what I'd said before he looked blank. Then, not really...

He stared.

Only momentarily.

As though a dying bhairu was looking accusingly at me before lying still. Dead amidst those dried chinar leaves.

Chapter 9

I banged my head on the ground. Throwing it back and forth.
Repeatedly.

Desperate to submerge it, bury it, little realizing that the earth follows a sordid rule—it doesn't quite readily absorb the living.

I clasped the earth, holding on to those remains. Mourning Shukoh's death without moving his form into the inner folds of the earth. Lying on all fours. Lying still. Then not so. Licking its crust with the end of my tongue. As a child, hadn't I settled my calcium cravings through those walls of my Bareilly home?

※

As Shukoh's dead eyes looked accusingly at me—if not for

anything but a quick burial, I looked around, rattled. Bury how? Bury where? Those graveyards of Bareilly were miles away. And here, along this stretch, there were no qabristans in sight.

Throwing chinar leaves on his dead form and picking up half-heartedly that mass he was still clutching on to, I stared at the wilderness around me. No burial cries. All I could hear were my own cries. Then not even that. It was a strange vacuum that was overpowering. Setting forth fears and apprehensions of the wildest order—of being devoured by one of the lurking forms or dug into the earth or flung into a newly scooped-out grave or into a stranger's lap.

I pushed myself closer to the wet mud, clinging to it and then, almost simultaneously, digging my teeth into it. Unabatedly craving calcium. As a child, hadn't I scratched at the cement on the walls or crunched those eggshells, or gone about pulling out mud from the flowerpots lined up along the portico of our Bareilly home? And each time my father had picked me up from the floor with some sort of a subdued scream directed solely towards my mother, 'She's craving calcium…she can't walk forward, has one foot going backward…look at her! She's living in the past or what?'

He'd throw about more words along the same strain till my mother would retort, 'She's just like you!' and inevitably smack me across my face followed by another two, till I'd vomit out that still-not-quite-cemented cluster from my mouth.

My father would fume and rush off towards those

mango trees on the land stretching around our home. He'd return after a stretch only to get further lost in those nostalgic offshoots.

※

I carried on moving, crawling, finding my way like an animal moving along on sheer instinct. Leaving a bloody trail. I wasn't sure of where I was headed. Yet I was going on…just like he'd told me to. There was something so overpowering about this stretch—the full flow of Sufis and Saiyyads from as far as Iran, Iraq, Central Asia and even further down this terrain.

My clothes were in further tatters now. I looked around desperately for an escape route. Moving towards the adjoining shrubs, I stopped as suddenly those scurrying figures at that one end of the expanse reminded me of a marriage procession. As though wazas and non-wazas had assembled somewhere out there. For a marriage procession. But that procession couldn't possibly have been mine, for the simple reason that Meer hadn't married me. Soon, hazy images of a burial procession were somehow superimposed on images of that marriage procession. Marriage and burials—they follow a sequence, a pattern, a consequence of sorts.

I was suddenly jolted by the sudden spurt in firing. I sat back still amidst the wild shrubs. My hands were trembling. My fingers were no longer still. I wept bitterly, writhing in pain, recalling the last time my fingers had moved on their own. In the midst of that crackdown night.

Even as I sat hopelessly in the shrubbery, I pulled my face away and craned my neck to look through the boulders. From that semi-slumped posture to a more attentive one. I sat up and touched my throbbing forehead. I tore off part of my tattered clothing and tried to stuff it inside me, but it seemed reluctant to go inwards. I tried to stuff it yet again, almost cajoling it to comply, but out it fell. As though the rag was screaming at me—no, I will not go up that smelly leaky cavity of yours.

I sat still for a while, then started crawling, but giving up again, I threw myself between some shrubbery sprouting half-heartedly from between those boulders. As I sat huddled with that heap clutched to me, I glanced down at my small-sized breasts. They had always been underdeveloped, much in keeping with the rest of my body, but now they looked shrunk and under strain. I placed that wrapped-up heap of flesh and bones between those boulders as though this could be a place to throw it away. As I fiddled with that hole-riddled sheet containing it, I recalled Shukoh muttering that the remains needed to be buried. But buried where? A child's remains. Whose child?

I felt those remains. That mass of flesh and bones, maybe already rotting into nothingness. Life had been pumped into it somewhere in the midst of a lustful release of sorts, or during the course of a full-fledged lovemaking session atop a big wide bed, or along those barricades, or in those lush green fields, or probably next to a graveyard, or under the chinar trees, or by the side of wild shrubs.

Wondering whose baby it was...couldn't have been that half-widow's, for she had died during that search of her dunga. Couldn't have been that waza's, for he looked rather outdated and was well tucked in Sopore within the folds of the apple-producing belt of the Valley. Couldn't have been of any of the women who had hovered around that embankment, for why would they go about dumping their babies here and there? I clutched it closer, looking at it with a strange intensity. Could it be mine? No, couldn't be mine. For Meer would be taking care of our baby, maybe reading aloud passages from his books or quite simply talking about this or that.

I pulled my tattered clothes closer together and with that wrapped-up heap crawled along the boulders...to the other end where the goats stood reduced in a huddled format with their eyes darting about here and there, as though aware of the finality in the strains. I pushed myself into their midst, fiddling nervously with those remains clutched close to my chest. I flattened several strangely-shaped insects till one of them spat its blood on what seemed one of its own, also stranded amidst this hopelessness. I rubbed my eyes and gazed at the expanse. Wondering amidst this wandering...

Where could I head? Even if I could somehow crawl out of this mess, where would I go searching for Meer? Would the locals let me go about peeping into their dwellings? Why would they let these tatters have their way...these tatters on an outsider?

Maybe if I could find waza Ahad's whereabouts... but would he keep me in this condition? Wouldn't he be hounded for giving shelter to an outsider? Wouldn't those informers concoct and carry tales from here to there? A non-Kashmiri with a Kashmiri would have both—a head and a tail to that tale.

Chapter 10

I suddenly spot a limbless form in front of me. Another springing from an adjoining bush, stumbling at some distance. Leaping and grabbing another from that shrubbery. Within seconds, they had ripped off whatever they could find around them. Amidst cries, they threw those limbs around. One on top of another. Just about there.

Another one lurking, then fleeing from here to there, only to be usurped by a third. A fourth loosening himself from another's grip, looking about, totally at a loss. But only temporarily. Perhaps the parting not quite tallying with the extent of the want. After a second or two, even that went astray. Out with a full-throated cry of severe want, weighing down heavily with the totality of the weight and the additional freight of low density cries strangely erupting, and spreading out in the stillness of this expanse.

Gasping, outstretching, pulling the tresses hanging

helplessly down. As another definite form showed up... started creeping and coming closer...through that haze.

Right there. Right here. Right next to me.

Pressurizing me. Moving about rather too effortlessly in and around me. Muttering he was officially trained to go about checking and re-checking suspicious-looking forms—human or otherwise.

'These...what are these?'

'My chest! Breasts, my breasts, don't touch.'

'You're a woman? This bundle—what is it? Open it. Your child or what?'

'My child!'

'What is this heap?' He threw off those shreds that covered the heap of bones and flesh I was clutching. 'Killed your own child, huh? Twisted and...'

'Where's my child?'

'You killed it!'

'No...where's mine, my child?'

He fiddled with the remains next to me, pressing my stomach to make sure it was flattened, sapping it of the minutest traces of growth—fibrous, human or sheer synthetic.

'You have a child in this bundle with you. Wouldn't throw you for murder...here—revive this one...this baby... here with me...look here...at this newborn.'

Flow of words slowed down as peculiar smells gained ground around us. The darkness provided a cover to all those wounds and injuries—self-inflicted or otherwise, but those smells, unmistakably that of human rot, which no other odour can equal. Coming somewhat from what seemed like a newborn. He pushed it closer and still closer to me. 'Another woman's…this newborn…born from her…wasn't from my side of Bengal but a Bengali all right!'

He clasped the mass of flesh, bringing it close to his face, rubbing his cheek against it and compounding words to full-blown sentences. 'You're a woman—here, feed it. Here, this one…take it. I won't touch you—will let you go.'

He pushed the mass towards me, causing upheavals on my chest. 'This baby's mine…somehow found this Bengali here in the midst of this madness. I don't touch just any woman!'

He started groping me—turning and twisting my arms and legs. As though each segment was an offshoot of a terrorist or an informer who had nothing further to leak, contain or concoct.

'Was on VVIP duty. They do things in different ways. That saala minister, poking them from upstairs and downstairs. He with his lungi off, lungi pulled to one side…and then blaming the cook! These creatures do anything, everything. Converting, reconverting girls into full-time prostitutes. And then talk of paramparas! You…no, no touching you… nowhere, not even for routine checking.'

He thrust that curled-up mass of flesh to my left breast. 'Seen women…everything out for those top men. One kicking that minister right there. He talking of doing big things but saala was doing nothing for her! She walked out throwing those files at his chota sa you-know-what!'

He tried to repeatedly place the dead mouth to my drooping breasts, akin to midwives along with their medical partners making deep cuts, whilst inflicting trickles of news from those outdated medical bulletins.

My hands came in the way, ripping through the remaining remains on me. 'Nothing in them, nothing in me, not even a trickle!' I screamed.

I move my hands around, banging them here and there, but he wouldn't give up trying to thrust that dead baby's mouth towards my unyielding breast.

I stared at him in disbelief. A man who had no qualms killing couldn't force himself to believe that the lump was nothing but a dissolved assembly of stretched-out limbs that had an obnoxious odour, like outdated stockings earnestly clinging to a loose-fleshed woman. It was tinged in blue and lying swollen, as though all cut up, in keeping with the times.

One look at it and the memories I had pushed back into the past came back to life once again. All over. As those memories hit me, I started wailing for my child.

'My child?'

'Your child? You've throttled and bundled it up.'

'What're you accusing me of?'

'See this bundle, you're carrying this dead body…look, this dead child!'

'My child was pulled out! Pulled out by you bloody creatures.'

I tore off the remains of whatever remained on me. With my breasts unashamedly drooping like leftover chunks of meat at the butcher's. Like those rioters who had sat atop those trying to flee, pulling out the breasts as those forms lay about limply.

'Cover yourself! These are distracting! You've come far…are you married? Married here?'

He looked up as a helicopter made its presence felt right above where we were. 'Saalas—drop stuff from the heavens to disturb whatever little remains…are you one of those Hanjis?' he grunted. 'Worst of the lot, shifting around here and there carrying bombs. Speak up! What are you hiding? Show me your identity card!'

Casting a look of disbelief at that curled-up dead newborn in his arms, I said, 'It's dead. It's rotting. Throw it away—just like they snatched mine.'

'Where's your house?'

'Dunga on the embankment…my child was born there.'

'Whose child?'

'Mine. Born from me. Mine…don't touch me…I have nothing in me!'

'I won't touch you. It was just this Bengali woman—we never got married, it was just our bodies and minds together…no marriage for me! My parents married but they never mated—it was always just screaming and shrieking and shouting.' He put his hands together, pleading to some

Mother Superior, 'Save this one. I will not kill you. But I will be killed, kicked out of my job if I am seen here!'

I pulled him close to me by his collar. 'They pulled these breasts, pulled down my shalwar. I was hiding nothing. Nothing to hide, nothing to eat. Only on Eid, he'd fetched some milk and...'

'Musalmaan? Circumcision mark...must be a terrorist!'

'He was no terrorist! He had books and newspapers stacked all over. He had no money.'

'Was he a beggar or what?'

'No, no, he was far ahead of his times. He told me that they would ask for my name and religion at check posts. Is that what you're checking?'

He continued checking and rechecking. My sides. I tried to counter the moves to stop those pressurizing tactics. He touched me here and there, desisting from making any of those deep down penetrations. As though assuring me that in the all-engrossing task of checking and cross-checking he had remained tilted towards the East. So much so that he copulated with only those from the East or the Far East.

Chapter 11

He eased his grip from my shoulders. Looking around agitatedly, he said, 'Smelling...the smell's spreading, just the way it did in that Delhi minister's clogged bathroom...women flung around with that minister, crying...'

'Crackdown?'

'Crackdowns in New Delhi? No, no, no...not there! There are crackdowns only here, where suspects are dug out and killed. I was there on deputation. What all I saw there...and kept seeing! That Delhi minister lied—saala slept with Bangla women who came to him begging for the release of their undertrial sons.'

'You were with him?'

He looked utterly disgusted. 'I had to stand there protecting his legs as he went about demolishing theirs and spreading infections. The old fellow had difficulty raising a pyramid of an erection with those mummies huddled by his side. Four or five by his side always. Those partings of their legs couldn't get them back their sons—only got them infections, rotting skin and…'

'Circumcision prevents infections,' I said timidly.

'What?'

'He told me and…'

'That fucking man's fucking legs should be torn apart!'

'Are you circumcised?'

'What? Me? Bimal Basu? I'm not a bloody cut-up Musalmaan! I kill each one of them. Kill them when they've vomited all out of their bellies!'

'But this…'

'This one was born…just born. That Bengali woman's, not yours!'

'Mine? Not mine! Mine is where?'

He pushed my hands away. 'Day and night living on high alert. Checking!'

'Have you been checking circumcision marks?'

'No marks or remarks! Skulls, skullcaps…in yesterday's search those bitches started off—calling us semen-sucking bastards! Thrust a rifle butt right up there. Found that saala boat but all khaali. No men, no women…this informer cheated us! Today I will spare you if you save this one…a newborn cannot eat rice grains!'

'Whose baby is this?'

'That Bengali's.'

'With you?'

'Now gone—fled or dead or using god-only-knows-what survival tactics—Meena or Mehjabeen, going about changing names, hopping around here and there.'

'Infected?'

'Infected!'

'Circumcision prevents that!'

'Chutiya rubbish…chutiyapa!'

'Why're you swearing like this? In our…'

'Get moving. Out…out.'

'Where?'

'Out of here. Go back to wherever you've come from.'

'I have nobody there anymore. They're all dead in those riots—only bones, skeletons in graves…buried in those qabristans.'

'You're a Musalmaan?'

He banged his head on my chest, pushing me back, then holding me tight once again. He tightened his clasp and then with a maddening outburst, terrifying the body with uncontrolled fury, he ripped off the remains of those shreds that came in the way and violently parted my legs. He quickly unzipped his trousers and held up his drooping organ. It drooped further, refusing to getting perked up—remaining limp like a reptile in severe hibernation or a recluse. Sad and sullen. Cut up and cross. Like one of those leftover meaty shreds, gosht-ka-lothras, those butchers recklessly fling about, upsetting that cluster of flies that flit along with it.

'Planning mass wonders! Like her, looking for some

bloated sperms! Out! Get out of here now!'

'Where to? In these tatters?'

'No burqa here!'

'Checking…why're you checking like this?'

'Women can't be cut up there!'

'But you?'

'Me…what? Me what? Me Bimal Basu. I've done my college. What about you?'

'Postgraduate and…'

'Postgraduate and living with these bloody locals?'

'He was circumcised, not infected! And you?'

'Me infected? When? How? Wasn't even born here! West Bengal is my home, my mother was not infected. But it's not impossible because my father died of infection years ago.'

'From him to her, then to you.'

'Impossible! No infection here. My mother died of sorrow, not infection. The two had nothing in common, not even a common bed—he slept on the bed and she lay on the mat. Not to mate. No, she never went near that row of ministers who'd come for his funeral, hated those men.'

'Your father was some sort of politician?'

'One of their close aides…she hated him, even when dead and shrivelled-up he lay. They were total opposites. The only time they were together was when they were checking fish fins, otherwise they were far away from each other. She always looked at him in anger and disgust. She hated these politicians and all those connected to them. She hated his ways, threw away all his underwear and vests and towels and shirts in a big heap. Kicked them aside as though kicking aside his shrivelled frame. She'd call him fixer, pimp and what not… She'd died years after his death with a heavy shawl on herself, not one of ours but a thickly embroidered Kashmiri one. One season she wanted to give up, but the next she looked charged up. She had changed. She was no longer miserable, not even when this biology degree led me to protecting limbs.'

His eyes grew wilder. 'Dead…both dead. She didn't drop a single tear when my father lay shrivelled-up but went mad when that seller didn't come that season. She'd go running to the front door whenever a bicycle braked with that shawl on her shoulders…that shawl burning away with her.'

Looking lost, he carried on, 'Many seasons before her death she'd already fled…her mind had transported itself somewhere—she spoke of mountain ranges and peaks and what not…'

There were strange murmurs along an offloading strain, 'Even when nobody touched shawls in Calcutta's humidity, she went about covering herself with one. It's just that one shawl that kept her going…the only one left from that earlier embroidered stack. She touching the patterns webbed in it, saying that he'd embroidered it himself, saying that apricots and apples have little significance, or even the floating gardens or saffron blooms or tulip rows, when packs of wolves hound the sellers, the weavers, the embroiderers.

Don't know what she'd keep saying...and then dying with that heap on her.'

He went about offloading more and some more—he had been recently transferred to the Anti-conversion Cell to control overnight conversions of suspicious-looking forms somersaulting from one slot to the other. 'Out of sheer compulsion, the Khans sneaking into the Kaul folds or those Shahs creeping into the Shahenshah strongholds.'

'Are you from some agency trying to find out things?'

'Right now I am just trying to save this newborn.' He pulled at my breasts, yet again pushing the dead baby's face to my unyielding nipples. 'Why is it not opening the mouth?' he said, looking nervously at the limp form.

'Because it is dead!' I said yet again.

'But just born...just...'

He poked his forefinger on my drooping back as the voices of security men came into hearing. He pulled me and pushed himself ahead. 'Can't be seen in these shrubs...run... run from here...take this Bengali's child too.'

'Run where?'

'Run away...run!'

'Run where?' I asked again urgently.

He thrust his fingers into my mouth to block my screams and quickly threw himself into the shrubbery and disappeared into it.

I realized that I was now saddled with the weight of two dead forms.

One at my chest.

The other bundled up lying close by.
Bloated sperms. Bloated at some stage, but now lying dead.

Chapter 12

Before I could cry out or even crawl ahead, Bimal Basu was crawling back. Right back to where I was. 'No moving ahead for me. The dungas have been taken over. They're searching them and ripping them apart to make more arrests.'

'Arrests?'

'Maybe that Bengali's been arrested.'

'Yours…'

'Bloody kept telling me that I was conceived here. Telling me—Bimal Basu—that I was conceived here in this Valley! Theek hai, my parents never got along, slept in different directions but I can't imagine that my mother would ever sleep with any of these locals.'

Heaving and panting, banging his hands on his fallen balls. 'She's finished me…this Bengali! If she sees me here she'll vomit out those fucking details. I don't ever want to be seen with her. She has ruined me, ruined my career… for months she made me hop around like a mad person. Imagine saying that I was conceived here! Bimal Basu conceived here! Imagine my mother flinging herself at some Kashmiri in these hellish wooden structures and then going and having my circumcision done!'

'You were with her?'

'Couldn't throttle her! She had a way of chatting in these curfewed times and I wanted to hear her voice. She was desperate to make these boats…whatever you call them. Kept saying that these boats were built by her ancestors. She's mad about this place, had stuffed herself into one and dragged me there for…'

'To her dunga?'

'She was staying in some rented one. I told her to set up a shed with some locals atop that range or along the Boulevard, but she wasn't too sure. Kept saying that they'd be wrecked during those crackdowns.'

'She's from your Bengal?'

'South Asian, she called herself. Harping that her father or mother or someone from Chittagong, then shifting to…'

'To Calcutta?'

'I'm not too sure about her story. She keeps saying that her mother hopped from East Bengal to West Bengal, and then offloaded some tale about her mother running away further and then reaching this Valley! Then she talks about her father coming all the way to locate that woman here. All too stupid but then it's her story.'

'Why did you listen to her tale?'

'Don't know. She's different—not like those Bengalis that the Delhi minister fooled around with. She's different. She'd tell me to keep my head still, otherwise the very flow of thoughts will lump together into my testicles! After hours and hours she told me that I wasn't conceived in my Bengal, but here in this Valley.'

'You believed it?'

'Madness! Total madness on my bloody head!'

'She knew you? All your details?'

'Na, na. Just asked for my father and mother's names and then gave me that stupid theory that I was conceived here!'

'But you were with her for...'

'I didn't want anything from her. Not even sex. But she'd sneered—no erection or what? Diabetic? Impotent or...? Her bloody jurrat! She spoke like this...this woman. All the while taking me backwards...back to...'

'Taking you where?'

'To where I was conceived.'

'Where were you conceived?'

'What?'

'Why're you looking at me like that?'

'I didn't want to hear that rubbish. She kept dragging everything to the past! Hell! She rattled me—one night saying I was conceived at the Nowhatta Chowk, next night at the Jehangir Chowk or amidst shawls or amidst rows of books...went running to Nowhatta Chowk...probing those old hotels, those broken buildings along the Jhelum.'

'Checking?'

'I want to run away from here! Do I look like I'm from here?'

'Maybe.'

'Maybe what?'

'Some sort of a mix and match.'

'Mix and match! What the hell! Sperms from here or...'

'You were carted here and there?'

'You mean adopted?'

'Maybe. Taken from here to there.'

'Wouldn't I know?'

'Maybe carted as a baby or a newborn!'

'But me, Bimal Basu? Do I look like one? Do I look like a local Kashmiri?'

'Maybe!'

'Maybe what?'

'Meer could tell.'

'Tell what?'

'Whether you're from here or there or a combination. He knew everything.'

'This Meer is where? Take me to this bloody man.'

'I'm searching for him myself. Crawling all this way to look for him.'

'This bloody Meer takes you backwards?'

'All over...without moving anywhere, he takes you all over.'

'Is he some kind of a Sufi or what?'

'No. He's just an ordinary person with extraordinary knowledge!'

'Tell me his house and phone number.'

'I have none. All I know is that he lives in a dunga.'

'Don't talk of dungas! You're making me mad! No dungas! Do you hear? No dungas. This woman ruined my head. Telling me stuff that I can't check or cross-check. Ma and that baap, dead! No, no. I could not have been conceived here!'

'Your mother and father came here?'

'Faltu talk! I had come here once with Ma and that baap during saner days when none of these faltu chits were required. Even here, they went their different ways!'

'One to Gulmarg and the other to Pahalgam?'

'No, no!'

'One to Lolab and the other towards Anantnag?'

'Stop dragging in faltu names! My baap was coming here every summer with the ministers. He got Ma and me with him only once. Don't even know why, because the two of them went their own ways. One rushing to one end of the city and the other to the other end. My mother buying shawls from these local Kashmiri sellers, which he hated. I'm telling you, even when we came here, he went his way, don't know where…kept saying he had Bengali friends here but never took us to anyone's homes. He'd just kept screaming at Ma telling her to shut herself up and what not!'

'Who were you with? Him or her?'

'I tagged along with Ma to those shawl-sellers. One called himself Suffering Seller! That seller was ordinary-looking but he had made complicated patterns. For hours my mother would listen to his tales, nodding and smiling. He even came to our houseboat. I remember going out to play with the ducks as they ducked their heads under the weeds coming right into the bedroom of that houseboat.'

'Could you trace that seller?'

'How to trace the Suffering Seller? She had even invited him to Calcutta and introduced him to her grandaunts in Darjeeling!'

'Are your father's friends here?'

'He'd scream when she wanted to meet his friends. I remember we visited just one home, some local's home here...one place where Ma and Baba went together without fighting. It was some purana structure on the slopes with almond trees around a waterfall. They spoke tuta-phuta Hindustani. They cried when they saw me, and cried even more seeing us go. Don't know why! Ma also started crying when she saw them patting my head. Ma held me tight as though I would be pulled away from her, while Father kept nodding in a strange way, telling them that I was doing well in school and all that.'

'Go there now and...'

'Those homes no longer exist. The place has changed. Those houses are no longer around. Not just KP homes, but Musalmaan homes all gone...gutted! Been searching all the possible places. We security-wallahs are all sitting ducks!

Not supposed to mingle with anyone.'

'Which mohalla? Muslim or Pandit?'

'Not sure of anything. Many children, many people lived there. They were looking at us in that funny way, peering at me and my mother…looking sad even when my father kept nodding. Don't know much but…'

'Meer would know. He knows every little inch of this place. He had so many books and newspapers and…'

'Books?'

'You read books?'

'No, no.'

'You have no books?'

'Going mad checking every little inch to find out where I was conceived…not even sparing creeks!'

'In that house…you'd said on those slopes.'

'I'm telling you those structures are gutted! Those people cannot be traced. Don't even know who the hell lived there—locals or someone seeking refuge. I'm not sure of anything! Maybe Father knew them well—he may have helped them to live in refuge. His political connections were big…very big. My head's bursting now. This Bengali was sure that I'm from here!'

'Maybe…'

'How can I believe this woman? Maybe she was planted to unsettle me. Made me have her child, she forced me. She hated the word bandobast, but I can't do without any…I am trained that way. What to do?'

'Bandobast?'

'Condoms. She hated the word. This Bengali wanted my child…a child in this madness! She'd go hopping about on that bloody dunga, shrieking that I'm making the condom seem like a rude robber and that none of those bandobasts are really needed. She'd scream—don't spoil the foreplay, because foreplay is all that matters—the rest of the stuff is just a stupid release. One night this woman told me to forget about all those useless intricacies and just be potent. Can you imagine? In the midst of doing all that, telling me that I was conceived in a place full of books! Now I'm going looking for all homes, boats and other places stuffed with books!'

'Libraries?'

'Here these locals have big, big libraries in their homes. My father was forcing one of these locals to buy thousands of his minister's books. I remember how on the way to the airport my father stopped the taxi in front of a Kashmiri's bungalow full of books and Ma sneered. After all, political rulers don't read books! Ma wanted to buy books, but he wouldn't let her. Said the plane would take off without us. He didn't buy a single book from that Kashmiri man, but kept threatening him, forcing him to sell only the new books…those new history and geography or literature textbooks authored by the newly appointed historians or that minister, but that Kashmiri fellow refused. He argued with my father, telling him that those new books were planted or slanted and fitted with bogus theories and lies. He discarded them and kicked aside my father's threats.

We missed the flight that day! We left after two days. We didn't go back to the houseboat but went instead to some government guest house.'

'You remember all that?'

'Of course! Even those two days when we were stuck here, he had gone about trying to settle or unsettle that Kashmiri fellow using his political connections and all other possible bandobast. He was out for hours whilst Ma and I sat in that guest house. I remember I'd kept telling her to take me towards that house on those slopes, but she'd refused, looking worried and saying that the family could pull me away. She wanted to go to that bungalow with books, but I pulled her back, telling her that it would be unsafe…what with my father threatening that fellow so much. Don't know why she got attracted to that fellow or maybe it was to his books. He had all sorts of rare books in those rooms full of bookshelves and…'

'Your mother never mentioned where you were conceived?'

'What! Who talks of this rubbish in Indian homes? Our homes are not some bloody boats!'

'But…'

'Who conceives in boats?'

'My child was conceived in there, born on that dunga floor…and pulled out right there.'

'Even that Bengali kept shoving stories into my head that I was conceived here! Here! How? She had no clear answer. Kept telling me that it could even be a dunga full of books.'

He slapped his hands on his face. 'Books! I destroyed that dunga. Threw away all the books stuffed in some bloody local's creaky boat!'

'What? Dunga with books?'

'Confiscated those books. The creature clung on to his books…old man didn't run away, didn't jump into the Jhelum!'

'Where is he now? Alive or shot dead?'

He looked ahead. 'My philosophy is plain. Give pain—more of it. See that man there?'

'Where?'

'Can't you see that man? See him cutting? Hold on… look there, that creature there.'

'Is it a dog or goat or man?' I asked.

'That fellow there. He'd have been sitting with his penis bloody cut off, but for me. At the joint meeting, I'd suggested that he be made to cut and chop. So there he sits, chops and sits and chops…no, not his penis!'

'Is there an open jail or prison there?'

'No jail. Look there—at that creature there.'

'Isn't that a dog or goat or…?'

'No. It's the man we dragged from that dunga full of books. Can you not see that man cutting and chopping? We've converted him—from a scholar to a butcher!'

'What's the man's name? Which was his dunga?'

'Wouldn't know.'

'I was living in one, with one…'

'Name?'

'Meer...his name is Meer.'
'Meer?'
'Yes.'
'Meer Jafar?'
'No. Meer Taqi Meer.'
'Who cares which Meer—from here or from there? Off with his balls!'
'You're killing everyone.'
'You're talking as if the East Indian Company goras have come alive to pass a verdict on Shuja-ud-Daulah!'

※

Sudden cries ripped through the expanse. 'No papers on this boat. It's vacant—no man or woman. Jump into the next and the others too...'

Bimal Basu disappeared in the midst of these cries. Shrill shrieks of a woman took over. Words making little sense, echoing and then re-echoing as I crawled towards the goats and their remains lying flat on the expanse. Those words hitting me. 'I'm only half a Bengali! Left over...just a leftover! I can no longer breathe. Throw me back into those waters. Just a leftover. My father's gone far away—towards the Bay of Bengal—leaving me here, carrying another from here, from the family next door...dumping me here and adopting that boy.'

Chapter 13

The fury of the raging fire at one end of the expanse looked terrifying. Its intensity spread as though it had just consumed the bones and flesh of several, and was now moving further ahead...like those invading foreign forces ruthlessly intruding into the terrain after wrecking country after country.

But this time it was not human forms but goats getting hacked at an amazing pace, and their flesh getting stuffed into huge rounded degchis placed atop burning fires with wazas and non-wazas at their frenzied best.

I crawled ahead...just a few inches, even as those images of freshly slaughtered goats in the backyard of that embankment resurfaced.

I shook my head, naïvely expecting that it would scatter those memories, but they stayed. Unmoved. Determined to linger.

Pulling me back to that afternoon when those imploring sounds were forcing their way out of those partially-slit throats and Meer was standing there protesting in that backyard. He could no longer witness the sight, but as expected, Shahjahan Abdul Ahad had stood ground. Moved or rather un-moved his neck like a rusted pendulum. And had continued slitting slender goat necks with mechanical precision. Amidst horrifying sounds, blood flowed out and amidst it, Meer had rushed into the dilapidated structure. Turning his back, he had turned to face me. Pressed his lips all over my mouth and then on my low-lying small breasts.

Even now as I sat huddled, I glanced at my breasts as though checking that the pair bore no resemblance to any rooted growths…I looked around as strange sounds continued to make way. I looked ahead. This time determined to steal one of those bhairu chunks, but it seemed that a few others were also thinking the same thing. Before I could react, a form sprang out of an adjoining bush, stumbled a little over the lifeless form that blocked the way. Another leapt from another bush and simultaneously grabbed one standing not too far. Within seconds, it lay fallen on the already fallen one. Ripping off whatever little clung on. Chewing and clawing, and then throwing away whatever remained. As though still not satisfied, it dragged another one from the adjoining bush.

I pushed myself towards a fat-bodied goat as though it could be a sort of a shield, but I was too late. It was overtaken by a third. And a fourth seemed to have loosened himself from another's grip. Maybe temporarily. For then suddenly there came through a sudden cry.

Strange sounds getting compounded. A wild human shriek. It was as though I could hear the woman's shriek that morning as she pointed at an ill-looking boy sitting at the end of the lane leading to the embankment riddled with those wooden dwellings: 'Semen suckers on the prowl! No longer carts with sluts in the convoys. These fuckers should know that Badshah Akbar carted along many for his men, to keep them off us!'

I continued to sit hunched as those images begun choking me. Cajoling me to find a route of escape. But those bloody clots oozing out of me reminded me once again of that mass of flesh pushed out and thrown asunder... perhaps to add a tinge of red to the flow around. Or else to be ripped apart to figure out traces of any official and unofficial longings. Or to be raised on controlled parameters to partner yet another hulk.

I pulled the tattered chaddar across my face as the butcher shifted position. I crawled near those huddled goats. Just then one was pulled out of that lot by a human hand. The hands moved about in some strange gestures as he began what seemed like chatting with it.

'Did you see my Halaal? My goat's tongue has already been pulled out, it cannot inform anyone about this place. Last night I killed Halaal's brother Jhatka... the lot got by that trucker and now cut up. Must be churning inside the stomachs of the new rulers of this land. Our land.'

He shook his head, seeming to mix popular facts with shreds of memory, and stroked another's head. 'These two eyes have seen more bloodshed than hundreds of warriors in Hitler's brigade…I cut hundreds of these goats, otherwise they'd cut me and my boys up.'

I looked at one of the goats nervously squatting and then suddenly shifting here and there, with a commentary of sorts in the backdrop. 'Crawling? Primitive all right, but the only safe way to move about in such times…our forefathers on the run went about like this. I too would run, but how—now I am in their grip. Survive, or they pluck off whatever remains of you. Ahad stayed back. Maybe he'd stopped killing. I just couldn't stand the sight…when Ahad killed you all. But now what? What remains? Nothing! They interrogated me for hours but then let me off—for what—to kill…to kill you all! I'd have never sat here slitting your throats, but these men can't do without eating gosht by the kilo. Their doctors call me mad, told me to get over that "goshtophobia" and so here I kill you all, whilst these people sit and eat.'

I clasped a big-bodied goat. Huddled close to it, caught hold of it by its ears, stared into its eyes, trying to figure out how trustworthy it would be. Somewhat sure, I crawled next to its belly. Safe and secure. As I slipped my head under it, the goat's dangling teats touched my hair. I snuggled my face next to them, absolutely close to them. The goat reciprocated, bringing all its four legs closer, as though determined to keep me under its fold.

And as I snuggled closer, I felt a peculiar flow of drops on my cheeks, on my throat and chest. I felt my tattered shirt drenched with secretions flowing from my breasts. I looked around expectantly for a suckling mouth. Even in one of these lurking figures, but then there seemed to be none. As though they were in hiding, running from one end to the other in camouflaged covers. I rubbed my hands all over the goat's belly, snuggling further under it, rubbing it against those dangling teats as each one of them reacted with sticky, smelly secretions. Initially a bit hesitantly, I licked those drops trickling down. The goat stood there rigidly—unmoving. Unsure whether those sounds came from bleating goats or frail human forms, I squatted on all fours like a goat just over with the strains of labour, yet holding back the last-minute wails.

I heard the butcher raising his voice every now and then, in the intermission of a few seconds, 'A permit, a chit to move around in my own home? An identity chit? It is as though it's a Parvana-i-Rahdari!' He looked down at a shred, probably torn off the phiran he was wearing and shook his head. 'A suspect? Me? But I've told you all about my life…that wife, mismatch of my wants and hers, of my likes and her dislikes, of my entire life with her, but what to do? She's no goat. I couldn't cut off her slender neck. She can't even breathe properly…coughs all night, so what terror could she unleash? She lies in fear of being called a terrorist and flung into those cells where the very stench kills. She wants to go back to her hometown, but she'll get consumed shortly, while I'll have to go on cutting and chopping. Cutting and chopping like those gora firangees doing… Allah save us from them! No, no mention of Afghanistan here!'

He kept murmuring and muttering all through. They sounded like threats that middle-aged, middle-class, medium-built husbands unleash on their wives. But there was not a single attentive wife, oversexed mistress or any of those insecure harems to hold him back or hold out a bait to appease him into silence.

In this darkness who'd stand by? Not a mistress, nor the wife and certainly not one from the harems. He continued mumbling as several goats stood bleating around him.

'Stand still. I'm no minister monster to kill, to slit through your bloated tummies, pull out your children. Why have a child in this madness? I had one…my youngest one…my little son pulled away by these creatures. Begged them for days and days…they finally gave back my little child. I handed him to Ahad to keep him safe. I couldn't even keep my rare books safely, so how could I have kept this little infant safe? I worried for my little one's safety. Wanted him to grow up in those orchards, eat apples… only apples. No flesh nor these chunks. Don't you know everything? Or do you want me to repeat those details yet again? I'm now reduced to Ramazan Yogi, killing one Akanandan after another. Killing and running these knives on slender throats. Things that I wanted to escape from, but who can defy fate? I was thrown back. Each time…back…

move your back…have to make those cuts.'

Startled, I pushed my head out from amidst the goats and looked up. My eyes darted around. No, there was no other human form I could spot apart from this man. I was taken aback by his prowess to make up for the loss of company. He could have been insane but couldn't be better equipped. Playing all the roles himself. Talking, reacting, countering and cornering. He continued as though there were several people around him to listen, 'This one's skin seems fungus-ridden, smells like the dead fish of the stream…probably didn't come here with those wounds but caught the infection living in these cramped conditions. Even my wife couldn't adjust with me. See, she's down with all sorts of infections. Sorrow trickled down to her bones, to her bony openings…now she's lost her memory. Good for her, very good, knows not those dying or living. Now let me cut up these pieces that will go down their throats. This one's ready to be cut, slit and…'

I couldn't hear anymore for some time. Several men appeared out of the darkness. Squeals of absolute delight pierced the night, together with a bizarre sight. His fingers were urged to move a little beyond the set terrain along the inside and then outside of that animal's abdomen. Its bow-shaped legs started straightening, fast returning to their original arrow shape. As he came up with a volley of well-whipped-up shrieks while feverishly cutting its flesh into long strips.

I raised my neck as the man continued to cut and chop.

My stomach started churning in slow rhythmic motions, cajoling me to part with whatever the stomach had held back so far. Before the mind could foreplay or interplay or even intervene, voices erupted from not too far. Together with a contingent of bones. A lull followed. Again, more voices—demanding food. And more of it. There seemed to be a flow. A constant one.

In the midst of it all he sat there, cutting and chopping and shoving the pieces in the fires erupting intensely all around. In between that talking to himself as though making up for the loss of human contact. Spotting another of those goats, he started, 'And you, old one, what're you doing here? Too bony? You—that one who looks like a refugee. Calling my wife a foreigner, a refugee. As though she was some rat from that eastern sector! Who didn't seek refuge here in the reign of Sultan Mohammad Shah? Didn't Ibrahim Lodi seek shelter here and didn't the raja of Jammu and Jaipal's son, Anandpal, seek refuge here? Anyway, why rake up all that now in these turbulent times?'

He cast another look at the helpless-looking goats. 'Don't stare like that...haven't killed you yet. Too much work. Still have some hold left, you know that boy Qaiser... my son's friend...he's in His Majesty's information and broadcasting service, carrying information from here to there. No, no, not from Pakistan or Afghanistan but just local territories. Touba, don't even mention names of those two countries, otherwise arrest warrants would be slapped on this head. Whose head? My head? My wife's? And mentioning Pakistan is okay where these politicians are concerned, but not for us commoners. In seconds you'll be rounded up.'

The goat sat solemnly as though it understood each word together with the emotions underlying it. 'I don't eat flesh…don't eat you all, but those men—they'd kill me if I don't make these slits. They call me names, call me insane, mad, a lunatic. They think I don't understand English. I learnt it from that tutor teacher…an Englishman who was hated by his own people. Blamed them for reducing us to this level, to this madness. Said he'd tried even Afghan women but never neared a white ass, said they were coated with pimples. Imagine pimples sprouting there! But he ought to know! What can I say, I've not been with any of those firangees! Never with any of the goras! Married, but all useless. She kept away from me for years…yes, she'd escaped from her own people! I could still manage but she hated it. Had to do it here and there. What else to do— after all I am a man, a full-fledged man. I always somehow managed to get someone or the other, but it was always only one at a time, no double-crossing. I'm a Muslim all right, but I didn't want to be saddled four times! Got another one, but these men dragged her away. She had no foreign blood, but they dragged her away. Don't know where's she loitering about now—my little son…my youngest now dead…'

He stroked another goat's head. It was just a formality before the actual cutting, much in keeping with the practice butchers follow, of stroking in a rather peculiarly affectionate way before sitting and actually striking that blow.

'Now, you're not from here…you're from the Frontier but I have to slaughter you…Afghani yakhni…touba, touba! Afghani yakhni they gulp down without much fuss but I have to think and rethink before mentioning my wife's Afghan connections. No, not a full-fledged one but someone with a good enough excuse to be on the run.'

He caught hold of the same helpless-looking goat, and without batting an eyelid, severed its neck with such intensity that its eyes almost popped out of those sockets. Killing it not in the routine manner, but like a newfound obsession.

Along with these sounds of chopping and cutting came that distinct sound of an intrusion. No, the intruder didn't look like an animal on the run. 'Touba! A human…a man! A man…a full-fledged man.'

He jumped up and flung himself right next to the form. 'Hunched like the others?' His mouth stretched in a smirk. 'One of the diluted varieties or one of us—circumcised? One of us! Strolled here from the upper ranges or what? Eyes opened with a knife, there's no brow. Today's menu from Lolab or Sopore? Ahad would know. Always knows. He's been a friend all right, but couldn't control that crossfiring in those apple orchards, those bullets killed my little child…my youngest one gone. Those bullets killed him…he was so young, just a few months old he was…now gone.'

He cast his glance sideways at the goats at the other

end. I sat huddled among them. I could sense his eyes darting around…under that big-sized goat I had taken refuge under.

I cried out as he focused his gaze on me. He spun me around, taking his time to decide which particular part would be best suited to be first parted from my body. He stroked my hair, much in keeping with the practice he'd followed, of touching his prey very gently before making those precise slits. As though verifying all possible problems, like a motor mechanic fiddling with the already fixed parts.

He looked shocked as his eyes fell on my face. 'A human face! Another human form from God knows where… running towards these goats for safety, for camouflage. This one's burdened with sorrow… sorrow, tears all over the face.'

He stared straight into my eyes. 'But you don't look like one of these wretches! You're one of the bloated sperms! Move on. There're security creatures feasting there. Sitting on walnut-carved chairs and… Quickly get out before I run this knife through you…my fingers on this knife are desperate to get moving. No, I can't kill mothers looking for lost…dead sons,' he mumbled, looking confused as to what to do with me.

Suddenly he pulled me back with one hand as those knives and blades clutched in the other fell freely to the ground. Each one of them falling…from his grip. Some falling on his slumped form and the rest on me.

The goat tried to break free towards the two other goats standing huddled together, even as voices were heard from not too far. But the goats didn't move, didn't react. It was either sheer forbearance or that peculiar intuition that animals have that made it known to them that those intruding voices were not heralding their demise, but that of hapless human beings trying to find escape routes.

༅

I couldn't move any further. I was arrested. With two dead children on me. During the search, the state's Anti-terrorist Cell found near-crumpled chits with two names—Husna Hakeem and Deepti Kaul.

The interrogation centre set up in the jail premises echo with my shrieks as they interrogate me. Even as I continue to mumble, 'Meer gave me these chits for my survival… here and there, elsewhere. Meer who? Meer sitting there—a collector of rare books, now cutting and chopping. The two bodies of those babies on me. Destiny's children…fling them into unmarked graves.'

Author's Note

Meer is a tale close to my heart and soul. For several long years I have seen and sensed the pain and suffering in the Kashmir Valley; perhaps these strains are widespread and can be best grasped by those surviving in other conflict zones of this subcontinent.

My debut novel carries an abundance of emotions of varying hues and shades. After all, one can do without mundane basics but not without emotions and emotional bonding. Without sounding clichéd, writing your first novel seems not too different from your first romantic take-off. You offload along the innocent strain, without dilutions and distractions, without those sways and sighs. Holding out those raw emotions, many a time trampled upon, sometimes fading away towards an oblivion of sorts, dying a slow, painful death…

I am extremely grateful to Rupa Publications for

publishing my debut novel. After Kapish Mehra gave the go-ahead, Ritu Vajpeyi-Mohan and Amrita Mukerji took charge, editing it with care and sensitivity and, yes, with much patience! In fact, I had come up with a long-winding title to this novel but it was Amrita who spontaneously suggested this rather apt title *Meer*! After all, he is one of the central characters and it is through him that the ground realities get relayed. Dark realities in these dark times.